"You're hi
can forgive
yourself," R

She crossed her arms over her middle and wrapped her hands around her elbows. "You're not being fair, Robert. Besides, since when do you have a degree in psychology?"

He moved slowly toward her. "I'm not a psychologist. I'm just a man who sees a beautiful, warm, giving woman sentencing herself to a life of loneliness."

She dropped her arms and moved backward as he continued his slow advance toward her. Her heart beat frantically as she met his gaze, the intense look in his blue eyes seeming to steal the breath from her body.

"You have a wall, too, Robert. You won't stray off the course you planned for your life, no matter what happens or who you meet," Winter said, her back pressed against the refrigerator.

Robert closed the distance between them and stood directly in front of her. He planted a hand on either side of her head and leaned closer, trapping her in place with his body. "But you're chipping away at my wall, aren't you, Winter?" he said, his voice very low. "You're tearing it down with every smile, every laugh, every look from those great big fawn eyes of yours."

"I'm not," she insisted. "Really . . ."

"Chip . . ." He lowered his head toward hers. ". . . by . . ." He outlined her lips with the tip of his tongue. ". . . chip." His mouth melted over hers, and she surrendered. . . .

WHAT ARE *LOVESWEPT* ROMANCES?

They are stories of true romance and touching emotion. We believe those two very important ingredients are constants in our highly sensual and very believable stories in the *LOVESWEPT* line. Our goal is to give you, the reader, stories of consistently high quality that may sometimes make you laugh, sometimes make you cry, but are always fresh and creative and contain many delightful surprises within their pages.

Most romance fans read an enormous number of books. Those they truly love, they keep. Others may be traded with friends and soon forgotten. We hope that each *LOVESWEPT* romance will be a treasure—a "keeper." We will always try to publish

LOVE STORIES YOU'LL NEVER FORGET
BY AUTHORS YOU'LL ALWAYS REMEMBER

The Editors

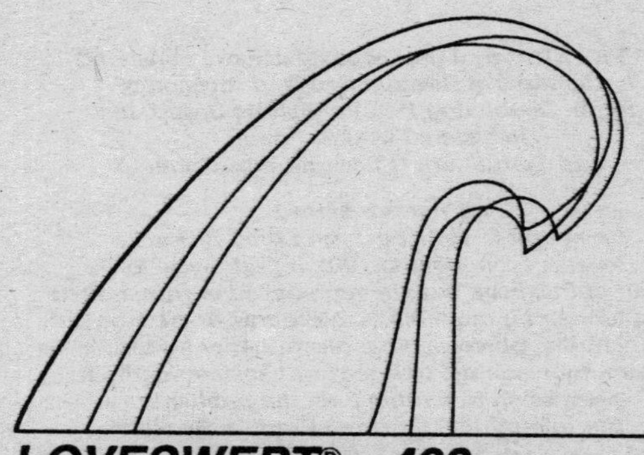

LOVESWEPT® • 492

Joan Elliott Pickart

The Devil in Stone

BANTAM BOOKS
NEW YORK • TORONTO • LONDON • SYDNEY • AUCKLAND

THE DEVIL IN STONE
A Bantam Book / September 1991

If you would be interested in receiving protective vinyl covers for your Loveswept books, please write to this address for information:

*Loveswept
Bantam Books
P.O. Box 985
Hicksville, NY 11802*

ISBN 0-553-44190-6

Published simultaneously in the United States and Canada

Bantam Books are published by Bantam Books, a division of Bantam Doubleday Dell Publishing Group, Inc. Its trademark, consisting of the words "Bantam Books" and the portrayal of a rooster, is Registered in U.S. Patent and Trademark Office and in other countries. Marca Registrada. Bantam Books, 666 Fifth Avenue, New York, New York 10103.

PRINTED IN THE UNITED STATES OF AMERICA

OPM 0 9 8 7 6 5 4 3 2 1

The Devil in Stone

One

"What in the hell have you done with my mother?"

The moment the harshly spoken words spilled out of Robert Stone's mouth, he knew he had made a grave mistake.

The woman's warm, welcoming smile instantly changed to lip-pursed anger. Her dark eyes flashed with fury, then narrowed, directly meeting his glare.

It wasn't like him to speak without thinking, Robert thought, but, dammit, he was hot, suffering from jet lag, and very worried about Bessie Stone, his sixty-five-year-old mother.

Now, due to his blunder, he was squared off against an extremely angry woman. A woman, he also quickly realized, who was one of the most beautiful feminine creations he had ever seen.

Her clothes were ordinary—a blue denim prairie skirt and a white peasant blouse—but they showed off to great advantage her slim, small-breasted figure. He was sorry she was standing behind the store counter. He wanted to see if her legs were as shapely as the rest of her.

She was tall, maybe five-eight, and, judging by her tawny skin, high cheekbones, and nearly black eyes, she was part Native American. Her features were delicate, and her smile—before it had disappeared—had revealed sensually curved lips and straight white teeth. She was perhaps twenty-six or twenty-seven years old.

And her hair . . . It was an ebony waterfall, thick and shiny, and he wondered how far it fell down her back.

She was absolutely beautiful, he mused. And mad as hell.

"Look," he said, "let's start over, all right? I apologize for being rude. I'm Robert Stone, and I shouldn't have burst into your store like that. I've flown halfway around the world to get here to Tucson, and I'm not even certain what day it is. I realize that's no excuse for my behavior, but . . ."

His voice trailed off. He was babbling like a naughty kid, he thought incredulously, but the woman, that sensationally gorgeous woman, hadn't moved or softened the angry expression on her face one bit. She hadn't even blinked, as far as he could tell. It was disconcerting to be attempting to apologize to what now appeared to be a statue, and enough was enough.

He strode over to the counter and smiled.

"I know I'm in the right store," he said, striving for patience and a pleasant tone of voice. "The sign outside says 'The Rising Sun,' which is the name my mother mentioned in her letter. I take it that you're the 'lovely young woman' she referred to?"

Silence.

"Yes, well," Robert said, "would it strain your brain too much to tell me your name?" Easy, Stone. He was losing his temper again, and that obviously was not the route to go with this woman. Was his tired mind playing games with him, or was she beginning to look vaguely familiar? "I'm sorry. You are Miss . . . Mrs . . . Ms . . .?"

"Holt," she said. Her voice was as unfriendly as her expression. "Miss Winter Holt."

"Lovely name." He smiled broadly. "Very nice."

"I had nothing to do with choosing it. It was my parents' choice."

"That's true, but . . ." Dammit, he thought, one step forward, two steps back. Winter Holt was not an easy person to deal with. Winter. It really was a lyrical name, although at the moment it was sadly appropriate. He was receiving an extremely chilly reception. "Miss Holt . . . Winter, if I may . . . I'm very concerned about my mother. You do know Bessie Stone, don't you?"

Before Winter could reply, the door to her shop opened and a middle-aged couple entered. Winter stepped sideways and smiled at the pair.

"Hello," she said. "Welcome to The Rising Sun.

May I help you find something, or would you care to browse?"

"We're looking for some earrings to match my wife's necklace," the man said.

"Well, let's see if we can do exactly that. If you'll just come down to the end of the counter, I'll show you what we have."

She moved away without giving Robert another glance, and he watched her go.

Her hair, he saw, fell nearly to her waist. Beautiful. What would it feel like sliding through his fingers? What would it look like as a dark, silken curtain concealing her breasts? What would it be like to touch Winter Holt, to hold her, kiss her—Stone, for Pete's sake, shut up.

He didn't have thoughts like that, lusty fantasies about women he didn't know. It was the jet lag that was causing him to have these R-rated thoughts. And it was his weary mind that kept insisting he'd seen Winter Holt somewhere before.

He shoved his hands into his trouser pockets and turned from the counter, his gaze sweeping over the store.

It was quite large, he realized, and very attractively arranged. The Rising Sun carried a wide variety of Indian wares—woven baskets, blankets, jewelry, pottery. Set on the outskirts of Tucson, the store was one of eight shops that created a U-shaped courtyard, with a bubbling fountain in the center. From the large front window he could see an enormous hotel about a mile away, and homes that dotted the foothills of the mountains.

It was all very nice and classy, he decided, and from the price tags he could see, the merchandise was expensive. The data he'd gathered in the past several minutes was that Winter Holt was gorgeous, The Rising Sun catered to well-heeled patrons, and Tucson was as hot as hell in September.

The unanswered question remained the same. Where in the blue blazes was his mother?

Robert wandered around the store as Winter took trays of jewelry from the shelves of a glass-fronted counter. The couple oohed and aahed over each one. Fatigue seeped deeper into his bones, and a throbbing headache beat unmercifully at his temples.

"The Navajos made these," Winter was saying. "They live up north near Flagstaff, Sedona, Oak Creek."

"Are you Navajo, dear?" the woman asked.

"No, I'm half Apache, Chiricahua Apache. I weave baskets, which has always been the Apache's specialty. There's a mirror there, if you'd like to try on any of the earrings. Take your time, there's no rush to decide."

As the couple concentrated on the wide selection of jewelry, Winter slid a glance at Robert Stone, who was strolling through her store.

So, she thought, that was Robert Stone, Bessie's Bobby. In spite of Bessie's assurance that her letter to her son would quiet any concerns he might have, Winter had silently doubted it. She therefore wasn't the least surprised that he'd shown up like a warrior on the warpath.

What *had* come as a shock was that Robert "Bobby" Stone was an incredibly handsome and well-built man. Bessie had been disappointed that she'd had no pictures of her precious, thirty-five-year-old baby boy to show Winter, but had gone on at great length describing Bobby's many attributes.

Winter adored Bessie Stone, and thought the older woman was delightfully refreshing, independent, intelligent, and full of spunk. But Winter had discounted half of what Bessie said about her son, figuring her effusive praise was the typical, sweetly prejudiced mother's opinion of her only child.

Robert Stone, however, was everything—and more—that Bessie had claimed him to be. He was tall—six-one, his mother said—and had thick, light brown, sun-streaked hair. His eyes were as blue as an Arizona summer sky, and his rugged features were handsome, not pretty-boy cute. Wide shoulders, narrow hips, muscular long legs that were well defined in obviously custom-tailored slacks, and the sexy, rolling gait of an athlete were all part of the package.

To top it off, Winter thought, suppressing a smile, the man had the nicest buns she'd had the pleasure of gazing at in a long time.

"These are perfect," the woman said, holding up a pair of earrings in front of the mirror.

Winter forced her attention back to the beaming couple, and a short time later they left the store, chattering happily about their purchase.

The door closed behind them, and the sudden silence in the store strangely disturbed Winter. She slowly shifted her gaze to Robert Stone, who turned to face her at the exact same time.

They were separated by the entire length of the store, yet Winter felt as though they were only inches apart. There was a nearly tangible, crackling excitement hovering between them, heightening their senses.

Unaware that she was moving, Winter slipped out from behind the counter and started toward Robert. He walked toward her, and they met in the center of the room in a pool of sunshine, blue eyes locked onto dark eyes.

Neither spoke as the seconds ticked by.

Robert filled his senses with Winter, the sight of her, the aroma of wildflowers that emanated from her, the imagined feel of her satiny skin and silken cascade of ebony hair.

Winter savored the scent of Robert's woodsy aftershave, heady sweat, and pure male essence. She envisioned her fingertips gliding over the shadowy beard beginning to show along his chiseled jawline, then moving on to the dark blond curls on his chest, just visible where he'd undone the top two buttons of his pale blue dress shirt.

Her gaze rose and fastened on his lips—lips, she realized, that she wanted to kiss, needed to kiss. *Now.*

Dear Lord, Robert thought hazily, he had to

kiss Winter Holt before he went out of his mind. Never had he fallen under such a sensual spell as this woman was weaving around him. He had to have her. *Now.*

"Winter."

He heard her name spoken in a voice rough with desire, then foggily realized it was he who had said it. He blinked, shook his head in an attempt to clear it, then forced himself to take a step back.

"Jet lag," he said, still not quite recognizing the sound of his own voice.

"Pardon me?" Winter said.

"I . . . um . . ." He swallowed heavily. "I'm really fading fast here. Jet lag, you know. It's very hard on the chemical balance, or imbalance, of a person's system, causing him to act, or react, in a manner not in accordance with his normal behavior."

His garbled explanation freed Winter from the sensual haze, and she, too, stepped back.

"Yes, of course," she said. "Jet lag. I've been a victim of it myself. Mr. Stone, may I suggest that you check into The Chiricahua Hotel that you see in the distance there, and get some sleep? You belong in bed." With her. Making love with her. What? What on earth was the matter with her? "Sleep. You definitely need sleep."

"Yes . . . bed," he said, nodding. Oh, yes, he thought, he belonged in bed. With Winter. Dammit, Stone, enough. "No. No, I'm not going to bed—to sleep, I mean, until I've spoken with my mother. Which brings us back to where we began, Miss Holt. What in the hell have you done with my mother?"

"I haven't *done* anything with her," she said, anger once again flashing in her eyes. "You make it sound as though I'm holding her for ransom, or some diabolical thing. Bessie Stone is a guest in my home. When we first met several weeks ago, we established a rare, instant rapport, and she decided to stay on here when her two traveling companions returned to New York. She checked out of the Chiricahua, and at my invitation is using one of my spare bedrooms. She's a delightful woman, and we're enjoying each other's company immensely. She wrote you a letter that she mailed to you in Paris explaining all this."

"Right. I get a letter saying my sixty-five-year-old mother isn't going home where she belongs after a trip west, but has moved in with, to quote, 'a lovely young woman,' and is enchanted with some store called The Rising Sun. I'm supposed to shrug it off, say, 'Oh, sure, Mom, no problem, go for it.' Like hell, Winter Holt. My mother is a very wealthy woman, and although I certainly wouldn't say she's senile, her advancing age, combined with the fact that she's been widowed less than a year, could make her vulnerable, an easy mark for—"

"Now you just hold it one minute here, mister," Winter interrupted, planting her fists on her hips. "You're insinuating that I'm some kind of con artist who intends to fleece an elderly woman out of her money. I resent . . . oh, that word doesn't even come close to how I feel about what you're implying. You are, without a doubt, the rudest, most despicable, insulting, arrogant . . ." She ran out of adjectives and just pointed to the door. "Get out of my store."

"No. If you'd keep control of your temper for one second and look at this situation from my point of view, you'd see that based on the flimsy information I had, the whole situation appears very suspicious. I had no choice but to catch a plane and get here as quickly as possible."

"And now what? You call in the FBI to take me away, kicking and screaming, because I kidnapped your mother? You're not only insulting me, Mr. Stone, you're implying that your mother needs a keeper, that she can't be trusted to conduct her own life. That's ridiculous. Bessie Stone is an intelligent, independent woman, who's perfectly capable of taking care of herself. I'm sure it gave you a tremendous macho rush to come storming in here to rescue the poor hostage from the hostile Indians, but you're so off base, it's a crime. Now haul your gorgeous tush out of my store."

Winter stopped and took what she realized was a much-needed breath of air.

"You're absolutely beautiful," Robert said quietly, "when you're angry."

"Oh, good Lord." She rolled her eyes heavenward. "Now I'm getting very bad lines from very old movies."

He narrowed his eyes and leaned toward her. "Don't I know you from somewhere?"

"Grade B movies. Good-bye, Mr. Stone. It has

not been a pleasure meeting you." She spun around and marched back behind the counter.

"Wait, wait." He crossed the room to stand in front of her. "I meant what I said, corny as it sounded. You're very beautiful, angry or not. Of course, I've seen you more angry than unangry, or however one says that. And you do look familiar." He paused. "Forget all that . . . for now. I'd appreciate your telling me where my mother is so I can see her and talk with her. That's not too much to ask, is it?"

She sighed. "No, I suppose not."

He smiled. "One more question."

"What is it?"

"Do you really think I have a gorgeous tush?"

Her eyes widened in surprise, then she burst into laughter.

"I really did say . . . well, yelled that, didn't I? I have a temper that gets away from me at times, I'm afraid."

He refrained from nodding in agreement. "That doesn't answer my question."

"I'm certain you've had enough compliments from women on your various physical attributes. You don't need my opinion to add to the stack. What I think of you isn't important."

Yes, it was, Robert thought. It was suddenly very important to him. Not a rating of his body on the one-to-ten scale, but for some unknown reason it mattered very much what Winter thought of him as a man, a person, not Bessie Stone's son. Oh, forget it, he told himself. Jet lag was scrambling his brain again.

The door to the shop opened, and a young

woman entered. She was obviously a Native American, and was obviously pregnant.

"Hi, Winter," she said. "I'm here, you're gone. Anything I should know?"

"Hello, Siki," Winter said. "It's been busy today, but I've managed to restock the shelves. Everything should be fine until you close at nine. If you need anything, you know where it all is in the stockroom, and . . ."

". . . and call you at home if there's a problem," Siki finished. She looked at Robert. "Hi. I'm Siki Nanchez."

"Robert Stone."

"Stone?" Siki's eyebrows rose. "Uh-oh, the jig is up. Does Bessie know you're here?"

"She's about to find out," he said gruffly.

"I'll just bet she is. Well, have a nice evening, folks."

"Mmm." Winter frowned. "Mr. Stone . . ."

"Robert."

"Bobby," she said, ever so sweetly, "my van is parked out back. If you'd care to follow me in your car, I'll take you to your mommy."

"My, my," Siki said dryly, "you two obviously hit it off great."

"Just peachy keen," Winter said. "Good night, Siki."

With that Winter turned and disappeared through a door beyond the counter. Robert stared at the door, then looked at Siki, who was scrutinizing him.

"Tread softly, Paleface," she said. "If you get Winter's temper in a rip, you're going to have your hands full."

"No joke," he said, striding toward the front door. "Apaches don't scalp people anymore, do they?"

Siki laughed. "Now that's an interesting thought. It would be a pity, though, because you've got a great head of hair there, sport. 'Bye."

"Good-bye," Robert said, and left the store.

Robert never noticed the spectacular desert sunset that streaked across the sky in shades of purple, pink, and gold as he followed Winter's white van away from the city. She drove along a winding dirt road that brought them closer and closer to the mountains. They were steadily climbing, too, and at last she turned onto a blacktopped driveway that led to a large ranch-style house. Made of burnt adobe, the house blended in perfectly with the wild desert that surrounded it.

Winter parked next to the house, and Robert pulled in beside her. They met at the front of her van.

"Winter," he asked, "can't we call a truce?"

"That's what Custer said." She started toward the house.

"Thanks a bunch," he muttered.

She was being so witchy, Winter thought as she dug in her purse for her key. It wasn't like her to be rude. She could understand Robert's concern about his mother, but she hadn't given him one inch of compassion on the subject.

And she knew why. She was too unsettled by the sensual effect he had on her. It had been a long time since she'd felt desire stir within her, since she'd been so vividly aware of her own femininity.

And she didn't like it, not one little bit.

She'd built protective walls around her heart, her soul, high and strong, and they'd held her in good stead ever since . . . No, this was not the time to be dwelling on old and painful memories. She had to stay alert and guard against the strange spell Robert Stone seemed capable of weaving around her.

She opened the door and entered the house, with Robert right behind her. A refreshing wave of coolness from the air conditioner greeted them.

"Hello," Winter called. "I'm home."

Robert stopped just inside the house and looked around the large living room. The carpeting was the same burnt adobe color as the exterior of the house, creating a sense of continuity between the outside and the inside. Rather than paintings, Indian rugs in bright varying shades hung on the pristine white walls. The furniture was rattan, with puffy, multicolored cushions in earth tones.

The flagstone fireplace against the far wall was topped by a natural wood mantel that held pottery and baskets. Smaller pieces of pottery and figurines dotted the end tables and coffee table. The side of the room that faced the mountains was composed of gleaming floor-to-ceiling windows, revealing the breathtaking view beyond.

"This is a fantastic room," he said. "I've never

seen anything quite like it before. But I've never been in Arizona before, either. You have a lovely home, Winter."

"Thank you," she said, not looking at him. "Hello?" she called again.

She set her purse on an end table and started across the room. A swinging door opened at the far end of the room and a woman entered. She was small-boned, and not more than five feet tall, with short, curly gray hair. She was wearing a pale green shirtwaist dress that had an expensive sheen to it, despite its casual style.

"Hello, Winter dear," the woman said. "Did you have a nice day at the—" She stopped dead in her tracks, her eyes widening. "Bobby."

Robert folded his arms across his chest, a rather disinterested expression on his face. "Hello, Mother. I was in the neighborhood, so I thought I'd drop by." He shook his head and frowned. "What's going on here? I've never known you to do something so—so reckless. I've spoken with your two friends who made the trip west with you six weeks ago. They're very upset and shocked that you refused to return home with them. The fact that I'm here should tell you that I'm not thrilled by your actions, either. This is very out of character for you."

"I'll leave you two alone," Winter said. "This is a private conversation, and I don't want to intrude."

"No, Winter," Bessie said, "please don't go.

Since I'm a guest in your home, this involves you too. Besides, dinner is ready. I'm just about to put it on the table."

"*You're* putting dinner on the table?" Robert said. "Who cooked it?"

Bessie lifted her chin. "*I* did."

"Mother, you haven't made more than an occasional pot of coffee in your entire life. You don't know how to cook."

"Well, I'm learning," she said, with an indignant sniff. "I've had some disasters, but on the whole I'm doing quite well. *And* thoroughly enjoying myself. I haven't poisoned Winter thus far, which is a feather in my cap. Winter dear, do you mind if Bobby joins us for dinner?"

"No, of course not," Winter said. "Let's eat while it's hot, shall we? Robert, you may wash up in the bathroom down the hall, first door on your right. I'll just go use mine and we'll meet back in the kitchen."

"Splendid," Bessie said. She spun around and left the living room through the swinging door. Winter turned and exited the room in the opposite direction, down a hallway.

"Hey," Robert said, looking around. "Damn."

He found the bathroom he'd been instructed to use, then made his way to the kitchen.

The room was even larger than the living room, apparently running the entire length of the back of the house. The eating area was through an archway to the right of the actual kitchen, and had an enormous bay window and a padded window seat. The desert was beyond the window, giving an impression that one was nearly dining outside.

The table was large, round, and had a clear glass top. The straight-backed rattan chairs had seats upholstered to match the window seat.

Bessie was setting another place at the table, adding a pale peach woven place mat as well as silverware, a plate, a glass, and a linen napkin.

"Mother," he started.

"I'm busy, dear. Sit down and keep out of my way while I get dinner on. That's a good boy."

Robert slouched down in his chair.

That's a good boy? he mentally repeated. His mother didn't say things like that. His mother didn't cook, either. She'd always had a staff to tend to household chores. His mother didn't deviate from a strict set of rules, a structured lifestyle that closely followed the social mores of her blueblooded, old-money standing in society. His mother, heaven help her, had slipped a cog. Were these the signs of rapidly advancing senility?

"Something smells delicious," Winter said, coming into the kitchen.

Robert glanced at her, then did a quick double take. She had changed into jeans and a yellow T-shirt that had a brightly painted bird across the front. Her hair was in a single braid down her back, and she wore white sandals on her feet.

She looked about twenty years old, he mused, yet there was an aura of maturity about her, and a sensual essence that seemed to shout the fact that she was *not* a girl, but most definitely a woman. A very beautiful, desirable woman.

But Winter Holt, he firmly told himself, was not the issue here. Bessie was. He had to get his poor, demented mother out of there, back to New York, and under a doctor's care.

Winter set a pitcher of golden brown liquid on the table.

"Sun tea," she said, not looking at Robert. "You should taste it before adding sugar. Sun tea is naturally sweeter."

"What's sun tea?" he asked, eyeing the pitcher.

"Exactly what its name indicates. You set a sealed jar of water and tea bags outside in the sun, and nature takes it from there."

"And chicken enchiladas," Bessie said, approaching the table.

She wore quilted mitts on her hands and was carrying a casserole painted with bright flowers. She set the dish on a tile trivet in the center of the table, then walked back into the kitchen. She returned a few moments later with a tossed salad. Winter sat down, as did Bessie, and Winter spooned enchiladas onto her plate.

"Help yourself, Bobby," Bessie said.

He placed a small serving on his plate, then cautiously took a bite.

"It's good," he said with surprise.

"I made it from scratch," Bessie said proudly, "following Winter's recipe. Winter, do you think I chopped the green chilies fine enough?"

"It's perfect," Winter said.

"Thank you, dear. I thought that tomorrow I might try pita bread."

Robert set his fork down and leaned toward his mother, fixing her with an intent stare.

"Wrong," he said. "Tomorrow you're not making pita bread. Tomorrow, Mother, you and I are flying back to New York. You're going home, where you belong."

Two

The silence was deafening.

Winter's gaze darted back and forth between Robert and Bessie. She wondered which of them would stop glaring first, which would speak next.

The seconds ticked by with agonizing slowness and in deathly quiet.

It was Bessie who finally took a deep breath, raised her chin defiantly, and said, "No. I'm not ready to go back to New York and the life I lead there. I've been in Tucson over two months now, and I haven't been this happy in a very long time. I met Winter the first day I arrived, and I immediately knew we would have a special relationship. When she asked me to be a guest in her home two weeks ago as my friends prepared to leave, I didn't hesitate for a second." She shook her head. "No, I won't go back to Manhattan, not now."

Robert straightened and smacked the table with the palm of one hand.

"Dammit, Mother," he exclaimed, "this is crazy. You have obligations, responsibilities. You're the chairman of a lot of charity committees, you have a Christmas dance at the Plaza to organize for . . . whatever charity you organize that for. You've been in charge of that for years."

"Too many years," Bessie said. "There are vice-chairmen for every one of these committees I head. Let them take over. It's always been good old Bessie Stone giving of her time, her self. Well, now it's my turn to do what *I'd* like to do."

"Like learning to cook? For Pete's sake, why do you suddenly want to know how to cook?"

"I don't have to justify my reasons. I want to learn to cook, so that's exactly what I intend to do."

Robert stared up at the ceiling for a long moment to regain control of his temper. When he looked at his mother again, he forced a gentle quality into his voice.

"Mother, please listen to me. You're not yourself. You're acting like a rebellious teenager. I'm not condemning you, I'm understanding you. But I think you should see your physician. Maybe it would help to talk to a psychiatrist too. It's been rough for you since Father died, and I've been overseas much of the time since then, seeing to the foreign investments Father and I had acquired. I'll juggle things around, make it possible to be in New York until you're—"

"Being a good little girl again?" Bessie interrupted. Her eyes narrowed. "Robert Stone, you are a stuffed shirt. You shove people into slots and then expect them to stay there and not cause you any upset. You have your life all mapped out, just as your father did. I loved that man, but I learned to my sorrow many years ago that I mustn't make waves, mustn't deviate one iota from Henry Stone's master plan. You're picking up exactly where your father left off, and I'll be damned, young man, if I'm going to allow you to control my life the way he did."

Hooray for Bessie, Winter mentally cheered. She was standing firm, and she was going to have her chance to be who *she* was, live the life *she* wanted. And, Winter thought, glancing at Bessie's son, the storm of fury within Robert was building with every tick of the clock. He was obviously, from what Bessie had said, his father's son in attitude and outlook, a person thrown off-kilter by change. He was, she thought sadly, a stodgy old man walking around in a magnificent, gorgeous, youthful body.

"For the first time since I can remember," Bessie said quietly, "I am para-ah-dee-ah-tran."

"What?" Robert asked, his frown deepening.

"Contented," Winter said. "That's Apache for contented."

His head snapped around, and he stared at her as though he'd forgotten she was there. Her pleasant expression further fanned his irritation.

"Wonderful," he said sarcastically. "I suppose my mother is going to learn how to speak

Apache along with her other nifty new endeavors."

Winter shrugged, then examined her fingernails for a moment before looking at Robert again.

"It's a fascinating language," she said. "The entire Indian culture is interesting, and has much to offer in the way of wisdom. I come from both worlds, and I find a great many of the Native American beliefs sound. Para-ah-dee-ah-tran, to be contented, is something to be cherished and protected. Don't you feel that everyone has a right to feel a sense of contentment in their life?"

"Not," he said tightly, "when it is obtained at the expense of others. People have clearly defined roles and—"

"Dear heaven," Winter said, cutting him off, "what about change, growth, moving into the next phase of one's life? Where do you envision yourself twenty years from now?"

"Doing exactly what I'm engaged in at the present time," he said. A muscle jumped along his tightly clenched jaw. "I've been president of Stone Investment Corporation since my father's death, and I'll remain as such until *I* die. My focus, the road I'll travel, is perfectly clear, as was my mother's until she came on this trip to Tucson. Maybe you shift gears whenever the mood strikes, Winter, but Stones *do not.*"

"*This* Stone is," Bessie said.

"Ah, hell." Robert closed his eyes and slouched back in his chair, squeezing the bridge of his nose.

A wave of tenderness swept over Winter as she watched him. He was, she remembered, exhausted and suffering from severe jet lag. While the issue of Bessie's actions and Robert's reactions to them was far from settled, there was nothing to be gained from a debate conducted now, while Robert was so tired. It could, in fact, lead to harsh, hurtful words being flung between mother and son.

"Robert," she said, "don't you think it would be best for everyone concerned if you got some rest? The snowbirds—the winter visitors—are due in soon from the east, but I'm sure there's still a room, perhaps even a suite, available at The Chiricahua Hotel. Wouldn't it be better to tackle all this tomorrow?"

"Winter is right, dear," Bessie said. "You need some sleep. We're not going to accomplish anything tonight. Why don't you go on to the hotel and come back here in the morning?"

"Yes, all right," Robert said. He stood slowly, weariness evident in his sluggish movements. "Thank you for the dinner. Good night, ladies."

"I'll see you to the door," Winter said.

She followed him from the kitchen and through the living room.

"Robert," she said quietly, as they stood by the door, "I feel as though I'm caught in the middle here. It was never my intention to cause problems between you and Bessie. I hope you realize she would have stayed on at the hotel if I hadn't invited her into my home."

He ran one hand over the back of his neck. "Yeah," he said, in a voice heavy with fatigue.

"She's definitely dug in her heels. I've never seen her so determined, so stubborn."

"I know you're eager to get some sleep, but I do have one confession to make."

He raised his eyebrows in a questioning manner.

"Honesty is very important to me," she went on, "so I have to tell you that I'm not surprised you showed up here. At the time that Bessie wrote to you about her intentions, I could see where her sudden change of plans could be reason for concern. My anger at The Rising Sun was due to your, shall we say, rather rude approach to the subject. I hope you're aware by now that I'm not a con artist who is after your mother's money. She's my friend, and I enjoy her company. Period. Do you believe me?"

Robert looked into her eyes, and she held his gaze steadily. Slowly, slowly, the silken threads of sensuality they'd felt at her store wove around them again, holding them fast. Desire pulsed and hearts pounded. Heat swirled through their bodies as their minds were filled with passionate pictures of touching, kissing, reaching for each other to quell the burning need within them.

Robert raised one shaking hand and drew his thumb lightly over Winter's lips. She shivered from the feathery caress, a soft sigh catching in her throat.

"I believe you," he said, his voice raspy.

"Thank you," she whispered.

"Good night, Winter."

"Sleep well, Robert."

He left the house, closing the door with a quiet click. Winter didn't move. She drew in a steadying breath and pressed her hands to her flushed cheeks.

She was shaken that she had fallen prey, again, to Robert's masculine magnetism. She could still feel the heat deep within her, thrumming with its insistent message of need, of desire.

No, she thought, she would *not* succumb to the sexual spell Robert Stone cast over her. It would be guaranteed heartbreak, splintering her spirit into a million pieces. He was just passing through, then would walk away forever, out of her world and her life.

Robert Stone, she vowed, would not crumble into dust the protective walls she'd constructed around her heart and soul.

She spun around, marched across the living room, and strode on into the kitchen. Bessie was still sitting at the table, absently poking at her food with her fork. She looked up when Winter entered.

"I'm sorry, Winter," she said. "The dinner is spoiled."

"No it's not," Winter said, picking up her plate. "I'll just pop this into the microwave and it will be deliciously hot. Here, let me do yours too."

As Winter walked to the microwave to reheat the enchiladas, Bessie shifted in her chair to look at the younger woman.

"I apologize for the scene that took place here," she said. "This is your home, your haven, into which you've so graciously welcomed me.

I'm terribly distressed to think that I've brought you trouble. I'll check into the hotel tomorrow. Bobby and I will settle our differences there."

Winter returned to the table, set the plates with their steaming food down, then settled onto her chair.

"Please eat your dinner, Bessie." She paused, then added, "There's no reason for you to move to the hotel. If you'd prefer the privacy it would afford you to go ten rounds with Robert, I'll certainly understand that. But don't feel you have to go on my account. You're my friend; I care about you. My concerns aren't going to lessen just because you're at the Chiricahua instead of here."

"Oh, thank you," Bessie said. "I'd better sleep on it, and decide in the morning what's best. What I don't need to think about is whether or not I intend to stand firm in my resolve to change my life. Once Bobby realizes I'm serious about this and goes back to work, I'll look for a nice place to live. I want to spend this winter in the desert, here in Tucson, not in Manhattan. I'll keep my apartment there, of course. It's really very lovely, and I'll want a place that's mine when I go to New York to visit friends. But I will *not* return to my endless committees and causes. It's my turn, Winter, and I'm taking it while I still have my health and enthusiasm."

"Good for you," Winter said. She took another bite of the enchiladas. "Your Bobby is not a happy man, Bessie."

She sighed. "I know. He's just like his father, set in his ways. He wasn't always like that. When he was a little boy, he was so filled with enthusiasm for each new thing he learned, so filled with love. And I'm not saying he's not anymore," she added hurriedly, "but he did grow more somber and serious as he got older. Henry was away from home a lot, and although he loved Bobby, he never had a great deal of time for him. Rather than becoming rebellious, as some children would have, in order to gain his father's attention Bobby emulated Henry—the way he talked, the way he carried himself, and, eventually, the way he viewed life.

"He's a wonderful man, my son," Bessie said, "but sometimes . . . sometimes I wish I could see again that joy of life he had when he was younger."

The two women sat in silence for a moment, then Bessie laughed a little.

"My goodness," she said, "I really did call my son a stuffed shirt. That wasn't a very motherly thing to say." She smiled. "But it's true. In my youth we would call a man who was so stiff a prig. Stuffed shirt wasn't very nice, but at least I didn't say he was a prig."

Winter laughed. "Either way, I think you got your point across. You're in for a battle, Bessie." And so was Winter Holt, she thought. A battle against the physical reactions she kept having when close to Robert. "Your son is determined that you return to New York and the lifestyle you've always known."

"I refuse to do so."

"Bobby is . . . uh . . . well, an extremely

handsome man. I'm surprised he's not married."

"Oh, he intends to marry when he's forty."

"You're kidding," Winter said, her eyes widening. "He's decided that when he's forty he'll just waltz out and find the woman he wants to marry and spend the rest of his life with?"

"That's his plan. It's so absurd. But frankly, dear, your statement that you'll *never* marry borders on the ridiculous too. I've been mulling it over since we chatted about the subject last week. One can't control the dictates of the heart. When love happens, it happens."

"Not to me," Winter said. "I'll never again . . . . Would you care for some more tea?"

"No, thank you. Winter, I won't pry, but I want you to know I'll listen if you ever want to talk. I sense that you've been badly hurt by a man, by love. But you're so young, so beautiful, and have so much to offer. You mustn't let the ghosts of the past control your present and future."

"I'm para-ah-dee-ah-tran, Bessie. Now! How about one of those sinfully rich brownies you baked?"

Robert emerged from the shower, dried himself with a huge, fluffy towel, then walked naked into the large bedroom. Sighing heavily, he dropped onto the king-size bed, pulled the sheet up to his waist, and closed his eyes.

Sleep, his mind begged. All he wanted to do was sleep. He'd regroup and reevaluate his strategy regarding his mother in the light of the new day. For now he just wanted to sleep.

As the welcomed mist of drowsiness crept over his mind, visions of Winter Holt floated before him in the haze. He saw her smile, could hear, in the foggy distance, her enchanting laughter. Her wildflower scent assaulted his senses; then, in the next instant he saw her dark eyes stormy with anger, her lovely skin flushing with the heat of her fury.

Then her expression changed again, and on her face, in her eyes, he could see the desire he had glimpsed earlier. A desire that had matched his own. A desire that even now, as he lay in an exhausted stupor, stirred his manhood to life, and sent heat coiling tightly through his body.

"Damn," he mumbled.

He rolled onto his stomach, punched his pillow into a ball, and drifted, at last, into blessed slumber.

His final blurry thought was that he was positive he'd seen Winter Holt somewhere before.

At midnight, Winter gave up her attempt to sleep and left her bed to stand at one of her bedroom windows.

She brushed aside the loosely woven curtain and gazed out over the desert. The night was nearly as bright as day, with the moon a bright, silvery globe and the millions of stars appearing like diamonds in the heavens.

There was such an aura of peace, of serenity

to the desert, she mused. It could be dangerous, could snatch the life from those who didn't understand it, or respect it. But to her it was beautiful, offering gifts for the mind as well as the body. Para-ah-dee-ah-tran. That was how she felt when she gazed out over this stark, harsh land and recognized its splendor.

But tonight, she realized with a sigh, the peace of the desert was elusive. Her mind refused to quiet as voices and images tripped one over the next in a disturbing jumble.

She saw and heard Bessie, who was determined to take control of her own life. And she saw and heard Robert, who so forcefully entered her life and tilted it off-center, unbalancing her, threatening her.

Robert. So handsome, with his bright smile. Stodgy, stubborn Robert, who had his entire life mapped out with no room for change—and no patience for his mother's quest for independence.

Yet this "stuffed shirt," as Bessie so aptly called him, evoked desire within her with a mere smile, or a simple glance from his sky-blue eyes. He was nudging her femininity, her sensuality, awake, despite her having tucked it securely away years ago. He was exciting, intriguing, yes, but he was also frightening.

Suddenly drained, Winter turned from the window and slipped back beneath the blankets on the bed. As she began to drift off to sleep, she heard Robert's voice once more, telling her that she looked familiar, asking her if he knew her from somewhere else.

Through the remaining hours of the night, Winter slept restlessly, tossing and turning, her peace chased into oblivion by the haunting demons in her dreams.

Just after noon the next day, Robert awakened, feeling totally rested, refreshed, and hungry. He showered, shaved, dressed in lightweight slacks and a knit shirt, and had an enormous, delicious lunch in the hotel restaurant.

As he lingered over a final cup of coffee, he was plagued by a nagging question: Now what? He was a man of control, accustomed to giving orders with the knowledge that they'd be carried out to the letter. He was organized, a detail man. Nothing was ever left to chance. His life was structured the way he wanted it, and under his command.

Wrapping both hands around the cup and resting his elbows on the table, he stared moodily out the window, but didn't really see the majestic mountains in the distance.

He loved his mother, but, dammit, he didn't need this hassle. Bessie Stone belonged in New York being . . . well, Bessie Stone, the way she had always been.

And then there was Winter. She was turning him inside out. She'd filled his dreams through the night, and had hovered in his mind's eye since he'd awakened. He didn't need *that* hassle, either.

So . . . now what?

He signaled to the waiter for the check, signed

the bill to be charged to his room, then walked slowly out of the restaurant and into the huge lobby of the hotel.

Winter, his mind echoed. If he could convince her that Bessie should return to Manhattan, he'd have the winning hand by sheer power of numbers. He and Winter as a united front would be unbeatable. Bessie would agree that she was acting foolishly, get on the next plane with him, and that would be that. Bessie's pride would remain intact, for she'd feel she had reached the decision on her own after listening to two logical people who cared about her.

Excellent plan, Robert told himself. Next stop, The Rising Sun.

When Robert entered the store, he heard a tinkling sound he'd been unaware of when he'd charged in like a raging bull the previous day. He turned after he closed the door to see a row of bells attached to a narrow, tooled strip of leather hanging on the door. When he again directed his attention to the inside of the shop, Winter had materialized behind the counter.

"Hello, Robert," she said. "Did you sleep well?"

"Yes, I really caught up. I've only been awake long enough to have something to eat."

Dammit, he thought as he walked slowly toward her. Winter Holt was even more beautiful today than she'd been yesterday, and the heated desire throbbing in his body was more intense. The day before he'd chalked up his overreactions to her to jet lag. What excuse did he have today? None. What was this woman doing to him?

As Winter watched Robert come ever closer, she realized she'd been waiting for his arrival since she'd opened the store hours before. She could feel the quickened tempo of her heart as he drew nearer, nearer . . . near enough now for her to smell his appealing aftershave, mingling today with the fresh scent of soap. And his eyes were so blue, so blue. . . .

"You haven't been to the house to talk to Bessie yet?" she managed to ask as he stopped directly in front of her.

"No, I didn't go to the house," he said, his eyes locked on hers. "I wanted a chance to speak with you first."

"Oh. Well, would you mind coming into the stockroom? My fall shipments are starting to arrive. We're heading toward our busiest season because of the winter visitors, and I have to keep up to date so I'm not suddenly swamped."

"Sure, that's fine."

He followed Winter out of the showroom and along a short hallway to a good-sized stockroom. Shelves covered every inch of available wall space, and an open box sat on the floor. The opposite end of the hall had revealed a small, neat-as-a-pin office and a bathroom.

His gaze flickered over Winter as she bent down to pick up what appeared to be an invoice from the top of the box. She was wearing navy-blue slacks and a white blouse that had tiny wooden beads of varying shades of blue across the bodice. The slacks hugged her small waist and slender hips, and the wooden beads drew his gaze directly to her breasts. He quickly shifted his attention to the box as he felt his manhood surge.

Winter was lifting a small black bowl from the packing material. She set it on a shelf, then made a mark on the invoice with a pen she'd had hidden in her hair.

"You have incredibly lovely hair," he heard himself say.

He blinked, then shook his head as he realized the thought in his mind had escaped from his mouth.

She looked at him. "Thank you. What did you want to speak to me about? I assume the subject is your mother."

He crossed the room and picked up the black bowl she'd placed on the shelf. It had indented designs in gray. The black portion of the bowl was shiny and smooth, the gray was a rougher texture.

"Interesting piece of work," he said. "I've never seen anything like it."

"It's a pot made by the Santa Clara Indians. No two are exactly alike. They spend hours hand-rubbing the surface to obtain that sheen. Consequently, a black-on-black Santa Clara pot is very expensive. People buy them for their beauty, as well as for an investment in western art."

"I think I'll purchase one of these. Are there other sizes and shapes in that box?"

"Yes, this order is all Santa Clara." She smiled. "Since you're going to invest in one, you should have more information. The original color of the pot is red. To obtain the black-on-black effect, it's fired for an additional length of time in"—she laughed—"sheep dung."

His eyes widened. "What?"

"It's true. I've seen them do it. They cover the smoldering fire with sheep dung."

"Dandy," he muttered, placing the bowl back on the shelf. "I can picture myself in my apartment in Manhattan asking a friend if they'd like to see my sheep dung pot."

Winter laughed again, then quieted, all traces of her smile disappearing, as she saw the intensity, the raw desire in Robert's eyes.

He closed the distance between them, his gaze locked onto hers. Stopping directly in front of her, he slowly raised his hands and framed her face.

Winter had the strangest sensation that her life was a whirlpool, swirling around, growing ever smaller and tighter in the center, until there was only space for one vision, one purpose, the focus of why she was here.

Robert Stone, and the kiss they were about to share, was the reason she existed, the reason she had traveled such long, sometimes lonely, painful roads. It was all for this, this moment stolen out of time. It was hers. It was his. Together.

No, she thought. *Don't do this.*

No, Robert told himself. *Don't do this.*

He lowered his head and captured her mouth with his, parting her lips and slipping his tongue inside to meet hers. As her arms floated up to encircle his neck, the kiss deepened, and their senses were filled with sweet tastes and aromas, as passion flared between them.

Never had Winter experienced a kiss such as this. It was a physical and emotional explosion beyond anything she had ever known. It was ecstasy. And it was terribly frightening.

Voices warred in Robert's mind, some demanding he stop kissing Winter, that he release her and never touch her again. Others whispered the urgency of his need, told him to go further, make love to the exquisite woman who was returning his kiss in total abandon.

Reason and reality won the battle, and he lifted his head. He drew in a raspy breath, then dropped his hands from her face and took a step back.

"You seem to have," he said, his voice gritty, "an ability to cast spells over the Stone family, mother and son."

She smiled slightly. "I'm not a shaman, Robert."

"Aren't you?" he asked, looking directly into her dark eyes. "Maybe you inherited more than just your incredible beauty from your Apache ancestors. Good Lord, Winter, what are you doing to me? When I'm with you, all I can think about is holding you, kissing you. . . . I want you, want to make love with you—but I'm sure you're very aware of that by now."

"Yes," she whispered.

"And *you* want *me*."

She hesitated, then nodded. "Yes. Yes, I do, but I don't intend to pursue it further. I'm not interested in a quick fling while you're here, Robert. Whatever physical attraction I have for you will be placed on the back burner and ignored. I trust I'm making myself clear?" She paused. "Why did you wish to speak with me before you saw your mother?"

"All right, Winter, I get the message. We'll put this . . . whatever it is between us aside. For now. I'll concentrate, for the moment, on my mother. I need your help, I really do. I'm asking you to back me in my sensible, logical reasoning that my mother return to New York City, where she belongs. Once there, I'll do everything within my power to convince her to seek professional help so she won't go off on a tangent like this again."

Winter stared at him, her face expressionless.

"I'm not saying she's crazy," he rushed on. "She's simply a victim of circumstances. The loss of my father, combined with her advancing years, has caused this mess, and it must be addressed. A psychiatrist or therapist of some sort will help her understand why she . . . ran away from home, so to speak. So, there you have it. We'll be a united front, you and I, and my mother will agree to return home with me. Will you help me?"

Winter continued to hold Robert's gaze. She waited several long seconds before she spoke, and when she did, it was only one word.

"No."

He frowned. "Why not? For heaven's sake, Winter, you can surely understand that my mother isn't acting in a normal manner. If you're her friend, as you claim to be, you'll do everything you can to assure that she returns to the ordinary, familiar life that she's always been happy with."

"I *am* her friend," Winter said, "and I totally support her quest for independence, her desire to see, learn, do new things. Her life in Manhattan no longer meets her needs. She doesn't have to go to her room like a naughty child simply because it would be more convenient for *you*. Your reasoning isn't sensible, it's selfish and narrow-minded. You refuse to accept any change in the plans you've made for your life. No, I won't help you, Robert Stone, not one little bit."

"Wait just a damn min—"

"And Bessie was right. You *are* a stuffed shirt. Now, if you'll excuse me, Mr. Stone, I have a shipment to unpack."

"Fine. You do that. You tend to your sheep dung pots, but hear me loud and clear, Miss Holt: Bessie Stone is going back to New York."

"And you, sir, can go straight to hell!"

Three

The remaining hours in the workday crawled by. Winter was convinced both the clock on the wall and the watch on her wrist were broken.

Each time she'd reached for the telephone to call Bessie and check if the older woman was all right, she had hesitated, then stopped short of lifting the receiver.

If Bessie and Robert were verbally slugging it out, and if Bessie was making even the slightest progress in chipping away at Robert's stubborn stand, Winter didn't want to interrupt the debate with a ringing telephone.

What was happening at the house? she wondered for the umpteenth time. There was certainly more going on than Bessie's first attempt to make pita bread.

Was Robert yelling? Bessie crying? Was Robert bending, even a little? Was Bessie making headway? Was Robert Stone going to haul Winter Holt into his arms the next time he saw her and kiss the living daylights out of her? Oh, Lord, she hoped so. . . .

Winter blinked and halted her chore of cleaning the glass front of a counter. She straightened, a soft rag in one hand, a spray bottle of cleanser in the other, and stared into space.

Memories of the kiss shared with Robert assaulted her, causing her cheeks to flush and heat to throb low in her body. Her heart beat wildly, and a shiver swept through her. As though watching a movie in her mind, she saw again the sensuous scene in the stockroom, frame by enticingly sexual frame until . . .

"And you, sir," she muttered, "can go straight to hell!"

Winter returned to reality with a thud. Spinning around, she resumed cleaning with a vengeance, the glass squeaking as she polished what was already spotless.

And you, sir, her mind echoed, can go . . . Oh, Lord, she'd sounded like a Scarlett addressing a Rhett. Robert had stalked out, obviously *very* angry, and that had been that.

What a performance, she thought in self-disgust. Her temper had gotten the better of her, and there she'd stood, yelling like a crazy woman, and telling the most magnificent man she'd ever met to go to hell. Wonderful.

The door to the shop opened, accompanied by the tinkling of the bells, and Siki entered.

"Hi, Winter," she said. " 'Bye, Winter."

Winter smiled. "Hi and good-bye. The Santa

Clara shipment is in. It's all priced. Some are in the first case there, the rest in the stockroom."

"Okay." Siki glanced around. "Where's gorgeous Robert?"

"Oh, well, I really don't know," Winter said, striving for a nonchalant tone of voice. "He could be anywhere. At the house with Bessie, or the hotel, or . . . Beats me where he is, because I haven't given him a moment's thought. Robert Stone hasn't crossed my mind all day. Siki, why are you smiling that funny little smile?"

"Because you are flustered, Miss Winter Holt," Siki said, beaming. "In all the years I've known you, I've never seen you like this. Gorgeous Robert has gotten to you."

"He certainly has not." Winter marched behind the counter and placed the rag and spray bottle inside a small cupboard. "Pregnancy has addled your brain, Siki. Speaking of which, how's the baby?"

"Kicking the bejeebers out of me, but don't change the subject. Winter, what would be wrong with your having a relationship with Robert Stone? In the four years since you've been back in Arizona, you've engaged in nothing more than casual dating. You're due and overdue for—"

Winter spun around to face Siki. "No. I have no intention of having *anything* with Robert."

"Why not?"

"In the first place, I'm not interested in a 'relationship,' for lack of a better word. In the second place, even if I were, Robert Stone is the wrong man. He's here temporarily to collect his wayward mother. Besides, we're too different. He's rigid, set in his ways, and has a master plan for his life from which he'd never deviate."

"Does he kiss good?"

"Like a dream," she said wistfully. Then she shook her head and cleared her throat. "Darn it, Siki, that's enough. I'd appreciate it if you'd refrain from mentioning Robert Stone again."

"I don't know how to refrain," Siki said, laughing merrily. She patted her protruding stomach. "If I was into refraining, I wouldn't look like I swallowed a whole watermelon."

"Oh, for Pete's sake," Winter muttered.

The door opened and two women entered. As Siki tended to the customers, Winter made her escape. All the way home she told herself to forget about Robert Stone—then her heartbeat quickened when she saw his rented car parked in her driveway.

Considering that the last time she'd spoken to Robert she'd told him to go to hell, she thought dryly, she was in no rush to go into that house. But, darn it, it was *her* house, and if Robert didn't care to be in her company, he could hike out the door.

As she entered the living room, Robert immediately got up from the sofa. Their eyes met and Winter stopped, feeling the sudden trembling of her legs. She attempted a casual smile, and knew at once that she'd failed miserably.

"Hello, Robert," she said.

"Winter. My mother is in the kitchen. I might as well tell you now—she's been crying. We had a helluva argument." He drew in a shuddering breath. "Want to know something, Winter? I can't remember ever seeing my mother cry before today, and I was the cause of her tears. I'm sure she cried when my father died, but she did it in private, with no one to witness it. But today . . . Lord."

"Oh, Robert," Winter said, her voice gentle, "I'm sorry. Did you . . . reach an agreement, settle on at least a compromise? Anything?"

He shook his head. "No. She insists she's staying here. I feel she should return home. We're at an impasse."

"Oh, dear. Well, I'd best go check if she's all right."

"I'd appreciate it. My face is the last thing she wants to see at the moment. I can't believe this. I made my own mother cry." He shoved his hands into his pockets and turned his back to Winter.

Her gaze swept over him, and she noted the straight set to his shoulders, the rigidness in his stance. She yearned to run to him, wrap her arms around him, and comfort him. The upset he'd caused his mother was so foreign to him, the sight of Bessie's tears so disturbing, he'd been momentarily stripped of his self-control, his power.

She raised one hand as though to touch him, then sighed and walked across the room to the kitchen.

Bessie was sitting at the table, her hands folded tightly in her lap, as she stared out over the desert. Darkness was falling quickly, and the vivid colors of the sunset seemed like ribbons of butter melting into one another.

"Bessie?" Winter said tentatively. She sat down next to her and saw that the older woman's eyes were puffy, her nose red. "Oh, Bessie."

"Why, Winter?" Bessie asked softly, not turning her head. "Why is it that growing, changing, finding out who we really are . . . Why should that cause such pain and anger in someone like Bobby?"

"I don't know," Winter said. "Perhaps because it's something he would never do. He doesn't know how to deal with anything that deviates from his master plan. He's very upset that he made you cry."

"Yes, I'm aware of that." Bessie looked at Winter. "My tears just suddenly started to flow, and I couldn't seem to stop them. It's all so incredibly sad. I'm asking Bobby to accept me as the person I now wish to be, but he refuses to do that. I must be Bessie Stone, of Manhattan, performing as I always have. My own son looks at me like I'm a stranger." She smiled slightly. "A senile old woman he doesn't even know." Her smiled faded completely, and fresh tears filled her eyes. "Oh, yes, Winter, it's very sad."

"Have—have you definitely decided what you're going to do?"

"I told Bobby that I'm staying in Tucson for the winter, and I meant it. If I give in now, I know in my heart that I'll never have another chance to strike out on my own. I'm very distressed over the upset I've caused Bobby, but I have to continue with this quest. I just have to, Winter."

"I understand, Bessie, I really do."

"My pita bread was a disaster, dear. We'll have to have leftover enchiladas for dinner. I wonder if Bobby wants to eat with us?"

"You put the enchiladas in the microwave, and I'll go ask him if he'd care to join us."

Bessie nodded and got to her feet. "I'm such a terrible bother to you. You've told me what lovely visits you have with your parents when they come down from Flagstaff, or you go up there. And here you are with a near stranger, a motherly-type person who is turning your peaceful home into a battleground."

Winter stood. "Now, stop that right now, Bessie. You're my friend, and friends stand by each other during the good times and bad. We'll weather this storm." She smiled. "Now heat up those enchiladas, or I'm going to pass out at your feet from hunger. I'll go speak to Robert about dinner."

When Winter returned to the living room, Robert was still standing by the windows, his hands in his pockets. She stopped in the center of the room.

"Robert," she said, "we're going to have the rest of the enchiladas. Would you care to join us?"

"What happened to the pepper bread, or whatever it was?"

"Bessie had a failure at her first attempt at pita bread, but she won't give up, I'm sure.

She'll try again, and again, if necessary, until she finally accomplishes her goal."

"That's cute, Winter," he said as he turned to face her. "A clever little subliminal message there to hammer home the fact that my mother intends to do what she damn well pleases, stepping over bodies as she goes."

"Oh, for heaven's sake, Robert," Winter said, planting her fists on her hips, "enough is enough. You're a grown man with a full, productive life of your own. You're acting like a kid who's just been told he'll have to go to a day-care center instead of staying home with his mother because she's decided to take an outside job. You want Bessie tucked away in New York so you don't have to worry about her disrupting your programmed existence. You're being terribly unfair, Robert Stone. You are, in fact, a prig."

"I didn't ask for your opinion," he said, his eyes narrowed with anger.

"Well, you're getting it, hotshot." She paused and took a deep breath, reining in her temper. Her voice was somewhat gentler when she spoke again. "Robert, when you were standing there for all that time staring out the window, what did you see?"

He frowned in confusion. "What did I see? Nothing. I was deep in thought, not passing judgment on the view."

"And you missed a beautiful sunset. There will never be another sunset exactly like that one, because each one is special, unique. You missed it, Robert, and you can't back up and have another chance. You didn't cherish the beauty of the moment, and now it's lost to you forever."

"The point of this sermonette?" he asked tightly. "I'm sure you have one."

"The point, Robert, is that Bessie realizes the importance of cherishing the moment. She knows that if she doesn't go after what she is seeking, right now, she will have missed her chance."

"Winter, she's too old to suddenly set out on grand new adventures alone. I'm being labeled as the bad guy here, the stick-in-the-mud, the—the prig. Did it ever occur to you that I'm trying to protect her?"

"As well as keeping her from disrupting your well-ordered routine."

He raked one hand through his hair. "It's so easy for you to take my mother's side, to urge her on. You're safe and secure in your home, your business. I don't see you chucking all this"—he swept one hand through the air—"and starting over someplace else."

"I did exactly that when I . . ." She stopped and lifted her chin. "Never mind. I'm not the one we're discussing."

Robert looked at her intently. What had she been about to say? he wondered. She *had* started over? When? Why?

"Robert," she said, bringing him back to attention, "I'm sure you've heard of Cochise, the Chiricahua Apache chief."

"Yes, of course."

"In 1871, when the soldiers wanted to move

Cochise and his people to the reservation, he said, 'I want to live in these mountains. . . . I have drunk of these waters and they have cooled me; I do not want to leave here.' That is what your mother is saying. She deserves the chance, and has earned the right, to find herself and her inner peace here, in this desert, surrounded by these mountains."

"No. She'd be alone here. She has a multitude of friends in New York. I know there are people there for her when I'm away. No, Winter, I can't stand silently by and watch my mother put herself in jeopardy. I can't; I won't."

Winter folded her arms over her breasts and uttered a sound, somewhere between a hiss and a cluck of her tongue, that was a clear indication of her frustration. She stared at Robert for a long moment, then threw up her hands.

"You are most stubborn man I have ever met," she said. "Stubborn, stubborn, stubborn."

To her flustered surprise, a grin spread across his face.

"Yeah," he said, the grin growing even bigger, "but I'm lovable."

"You certainly are not!" she said—and then she laughed.

She wasn't exactly sure why she was laughing. Maybe it was because when she'd been calling him stubborn, stubborn, stubborn, she'd had an image of herself as six years old, about to stamp her foot and stick out her tongue. Maybe it was because when Robert Stone smiled, he was too impossibly gorgeous.

Maybe because to laugh was not to take seriously his declaration that he was lovable—and she feared that perhaps he was.

Winter really didn't know why she laughed, but once started, she couldn't stop.

Oh, Lord, Robert thought, his smile sliding right off his chin. He wouldn't have been surprised if Winter had thrown something at him, or ordered him out of her house. The last thing he'd expected was that she'd burst into laughter, delightful laughter, wind-chime laughter, that was sending the heat of passion swirling through him as the blood pounded heavily in his veins. She was beautiful. And he wanted her more with every passing moment.

"Enough of this," she said at last, gasping. "I'm running out of air. Do you want to have some leftover enchiladas?"

"Sure. Enchiladas would be great, but . . . Well, I'm not positive that my mother would care to see any more of me tonight."

"Come on." Winter spun around and started toward the kitchen.

Robert followed her, and they arrived to find the table set for three and Bessie carrying the dish of bubbly-hot enchiladas to the eating area.

"Robert is going to eat with us, Bessie," Winter said, "but"—she looked sternly at each of them—"there will be no serious discussions at the table. We're all going to chat about things people chat about, and that's it. Understand?"

"Yes," Bessie and Robert said in unison.

The meal passed in an amazingly pleasant

atmosphere. The conversation was lively and varied. Robert reported to Bessie that Winter sold sheep dung pots in her store. Winter punched him lightly on the arm, then explained to Bessie the unique final firing used by the Santa Clara Indians for their pottery.

"Well, for heaven's sake," Bessie said, "isn't that fascinating? We could learn a great deal from the Native Americans about properly using our natural resources, about patience, and . . . Well, I'm a fine one to talk. I just heated up our enchilada dinner in a modern, quick, and easy microwave oven."

Winter smiled. "Don't feel bad, Bessie. There's a small microwave in the office of The Rising Sun. I use it to make tea or coffee, or to warm a lunch I've brought from here."

"The Rising Sun," Robert repeated. "I like that name. I assume it refers to the desert sunrises."

"No, not really," Winter said. "The word Apache means 'fighting men.' The Chiricahua Apaches, however, are known as the People of the Rising Sun. Naming the store what I did is my tribute to my ancestors. My father is white, my mother is full-blooded Apache. I love them both very much, as well as both of my worlds. I've never had a problem with a stigma of being a half-breed or anything like that. I've been very fortunate except for when . . . Well, that's all in the past."

"When what?" Robert asked. "What happened in the past that distressed you?"

"It's not important." She switched her gaze to Bessie. "Are there any brownies left?"

"Just enough for us each to have a nibble," Bessie said, getting to her feet. "I'll get them."

Dammit, Robert thought, staring at Winter, it *was* important. Something in her past had caused her unhappiness. He'd seen a flicker of pain in her lovely eyes before she'd changed the subject. There was definitely a ghost of a mystery surrounding her, and that lingering feeling that he'd seen her somewhere before. He didn't like it that someone, or something, had hurt her.

They polished off every last crumb of the brownies, and Bessie promised to bake another sinfully rich dessert the next day. Then she shooed both Winter and Robert from the kitchen, saying she could set things to order quicker on her own.

Winter wandered outside to the enclosed patio that was adjacent to the kitchen. Robert followed. The concrete expanse was approximately twenty feet long by twenty feet wide, and was surrounded by a five-foot-high burnt adobe wall. Padded lawn furniture was set around the patio, as well as an umbrella table that provided shade and a protective shield against the searing summer sun.

As Winter walked across the patio, she suddenly disappeared from Robert's view, as though she'd been swallowed up by the night. He stopped and looked down, realizing that he stood at the edge of the circle of light spilling out from the kitchen.

His heart began to race as he continued to stare at the clearly defined boundary. He felt strange, disoriented, as if he were on the edge of an eerie Twilight Zone. If he stepped across the line into that other world, he and his life would be changed for all time.

Turn around, Stone, the voice inside him, the voice he'd always listened to, urged him. *Go back into the house where it's safe. Go back . . . go back . . . go back . . .*

But then another voice whispered within him, a voice he'd never heard before. It was from a source he couldn't name, but it soothed his confusion and seemed to touch his very heart and soul with a tender caress.

Move forward, the quiet voice said. *Winter is waiting. Winter is there in the peaceful dark of night. Beautiful Winter . . . Winter . . . Winter . . .*

Robert stepped out of the circle of light and into the blackness.

He stopped again, blinking, waiting for his eyes to adjust to the sudden darkness. His vision cleared, and he saw the silvery moon and the twinkling stars in the desert sky. And he saw Winter, who had turned to face him. He closed the distance between them, his heart beating rapidly.

Their eyes met, and the now-familiar sensual threads wove around them once again, igniting the desire, the overwhelming want, until it burned brightly within them.

"Robert," Winter said, her voice soft and unsteady, "I just don't . . ."

"Shh," he said. "I won't hurt you. No one, nothing, will ever hurt you again."

Then he gathered her into his arms and kissed her. As he parted her lips, she met his tongue eagerly. Her arms twined around his neck and she pressed against him, filling her senses with his taste and aroma, reveling in the feel of his hard body, of his arousal, heavy and full against her. Her breasts were crushed to his chest in a sweet pain that became a yearning for the soothing comfort of his hands and mouth.

The kiss deepened, became hungry, urgent, as the fire within them flared, the flames of passion bursting free with an uncontrollable force.

Robert lifted his head a fraction of an inch. "I want you so damn much," he murmured. "I have never in my life felt so . . . I've never experienced anything like . . . Dammit, what are you doing to me, Winter Holt? What is this spell you cast over me?"

She shook her head, then attempted to step back, but he held her fast, close to his body.

"You're the spell-weaver, Robert," she said. "I can't think straight when you touch me. I don't do things like this. I want you, and yet I don't want to want you. I'm not a tease. I didn't intend to make you believe that I'm willing to . . . No." Her voice firmed. "This has got to stop. Let go of me."

"What are you afraid of?"

"Robert, let me go."

"No, listen to me. Please, Winter, just listen a minute. I know what *I'm* afraid of, and I'm not ashamed to admit it, to tell you. Something strange happens to me when I'm near you, when you smile, laugh, even when you yell at me. Then if I touch you, kiss you, I'm lost. My life is planned, but you're chipping away at that plan, crumbling it into dust. I don't know how to deal with that. Lady, you're scaring me to death."

Winter wiggled out of his arms and he let her go. Taking several steps away from him, she willed the trembling within her to still. Taunting echoes of words they'd spoken beat against her mind.

You're stubborn, stubborn, stubborn.

Yeah, but I'm lovable.

I'm lovable.

I'm . . .

"No," she said, shaking her head. "You are not lovable. I refuse to fall in love with . . . No."

Robert stared at her. "What?"

She stared back in horror as she realized what she'd said.

"Oh, Lord," Robert muttered. He dragged his hands down his face. "That is not what's happening here. Is it? Lord, Winter, we are not falling in love with each other. Are we?"

"Well, for Pete's sake, Stone," she exclaimed in an unexpected burst of anger, "how on earth am I supposed to know? I'm not exactly an expert on the subject. But I do know this: I won't stand for it. I refuse—refuse, Robert—to fall in love with you."

"Why?" he asked, perversely angered by her words. "What's wrong with me? What am I, a disease? A socially unacceptable person? I really resent your attitude." He blinked. "What am I doing? Why am I pleading my case? I don't want to fall in love with you, either. Not on your life, Toots."

"What a despicable thing to say! And if you call me 'Toots' again, I'll punch you right in the nose. I'll have you know, Robert Stone, that there are dozens of men who would give their eyeteeth to . . . Well, not dozens, but several . . . Well, a couple who . . . Oh, go away and leave me alone. This is the most asinine conversation I've had in my entire life."

"It's a beaut, all right," Robert said thoughtfully. "However, it's beginning to make sense. When one stops and properly gathers data, one is capable of analyzing the information in a logical, orderly fashion."

"Oh, shut up," Winter said crossly. "You're sounding like a stuffed shirt again."

"I'll ignore that. Winter, I'd prefer to take the stand that falling in love is a slow, gradual process, and that therefore love can't be happening between us. But I happen to know that isn't true because I have friends who went down for the count so fast, they never knew what hit them, poor devils."

"You're disgusting."

"I'll ignore that too. We have to realize that love, as much as neither of us want it, might be edging into the picture here, and we'll have to be extremely careful. I can't leave Tucson until I have my mother in tow, so we'll have to stay alert." He began to pace back and forth across the patio. "I've never taken on a challenge quite like this one before," he continued, almost speaking to himself, "but how tough can it be, how different from the business problems I deal with every day? I can certainly handle this. Hell, why not?"

Why not? Winter echoed silently. Sure thing. They simply wouldn't fall in love. But why did she suddenly feel so empty, so cold, as though ice were encasing her heart and moving on to her soul? Why did she feel tears threatening at the back of her eyes, along with an ache in her throat?

"Now then, Winter," Robert said, bringing her attention back to him, "do you understand your assignment, what we have to do? Don't let your emotions overrule your logical mind. Tell yourself that you don't want to fall in love with me, so you won't. With me following the same program, we'll nip this thing in the bud. Got it?"

"Yes," she said quietly. "Yes, I understand. I can see why you're such a successful businessman, Robert. Nothing keeps you from staying on course. My, aren't we fortunate to have a mind like yours solving this nasty little problem? Now, if you'll excuse me, I'll say good night. I'm very tired."

"Oh. Well, sure. Good night."

Winter strode across the patio and into the house. Robert watched her go, a satisfied, even smug, expression on his face.

He was back in command, he told himself. Everything was under control. Lord, he was good. What a brilliant mind. He'd taken a possibly serious problem and found a very simple solution.

His expression slowly changed to a frown.

So why, he wondered, did he suddenly feel so damned depressed and lonely?

Four

Winter opened her eyes, stretched leisurely, then sighed with contentment as she realized it was Saturday and she didn't have to work at The Rising Sun.

It was Siki's turn to tend to the store, the every-other-weekend routine having proven satisfactory to them both. Today Siki would begin training her cousin, Dulcie, who would take Siki's place until the new mother was able to return to work after the birth of the baby.

A baby, Winter mused. A tiny miracle. How glorious it must be to feel that life growing within, moving, stretching, changing daily until it was ready to emerge into the world with a lusty cry.

A baby. Evidence of the love between a woman and man, tangible proof that two people had come together in the beautiful, intimate act of lovemaking, pledging their love for all time.

Oh, how she yearned to have a child. It would have her coloring, she supposed, as Indian genes seemed to dominate. She certainly hadn't inherited a trace of her father's flaming red hair or ruddy complexion.

Yes, her baby would have dark hair and eyes, and tawny skin. But the child could be a blend of both parents. A little boy might have Robert's more rugged features, his stature, his athletic grace—

Winter shot up to a sitting position so quickly, she was momentarily dizzy. She pressed one hand to her forehead, trying to stop her spinning thoughts.

What? she asked herself. Robert's what? Robert's who? Robert's *baby*?

With a burst of energy produced by anger and self-disgust, she flung back the blankets and left the bed. Gathering together clean clothes, she strode on into the bathroom.

As she stood under the stinging spray in the shower, she mentally inched back toward her absurd thought.

Why on earth had she envisioned Robert as the father of her mythical child? She wasn't in love with him. She did not, in fact, even like him at times. He was a narrow-minded, stubborn stuffed shirt. A prig. He was . . . he was the most magnificent man she'd ever met, and when he touched her, she melted like ice cream under a blazing Arizona sun.

"Oh, sheep dung pots," she muttered.

Her vocal outburst caused her to swallow a mouthful of water, and she emerged from the shower coughing, sputtering, and thoroughly annoyed with herself.

Dressed in khaki shorts and a red cotton blouse, her hair in a single braid, she headed for the kitchen and a much-needed cup of coffee. She discovered a note on the counter from Bessie, reminding her that she was off on her scheduled tour for the day. A van from the hotel had picked Bessie up to take her and several others to Old Tucson.

The popular tourist attraction was a replica of a town of the early western days and, Winter knew, a major motion picture was being filmed there. Bessie would witness a reenactment of a shoot-out in the street, see cancan girls dancing and singing in a saloon, and watch the bank being robbed by dastardly outlaws.

Bessie was in for a fun adventure, and Winter wondered absently if Robert had been persuaded to join his mother on the outing.

There he was again, she thought, as she sipped her coffee. There was Robert Stone, taking up her brain space. There was Robert Stone, causing a hot flush to sweep over her entire body as she remembered the magnificent kisses they'd shared.

Winter narrowed her eyes, forcing herself to center her concentration on her final conversation with Robert the previous night. Suddenly clicking into his businessman's mode, he had approached the issue of their growing attraction for each other as clinically as he would a complicated problem with one of his investments.

Good Lord, she fumed, the man must have ice in his veins. He dealt with matters of the heart as he would deal with a financial challenge.

And the nerve of him to say that he did not want to fall in love with her. *Not on your life, Toots.* Oh, he was really asking for a pop in the chops. Not that she had any wish to fall in love with *him*, but still . . .

Winter plunked her mug on the counter and walked out onto the patio. To her delight the temperature was much cooler than the day before. It would mean a more pleasant outing for Bessie, and allow Winter to weave baskets outside, where she preferred to be.

Robert frowned as he stared at the closed front door of Winter's house. He'd pressed the doorbell, waited, tried again, and Winter still hadn't appeared. Her van was next to the house, indicating she was home, but for all he knew she'd been picked up by a friend and was long gone.

A man friend? he wondered, his frown deepening. A man more-than-friend? That idea did not sit well where it had landed with a thud in the pit of his stomach. Another man kissing Winter? Dammit, no!

Easy, Stone, he admonished himself. He was getting crazy again. He had no claim on Winter, and didn't want the sort of commitment with her that would give him the right to be upset that she was with another man.

Forty was his target age for love, marriage,

and a family. Winter didn't fit into his schedule, and he would gum up the works royally if he became emotionally involved with her. So, he wouldn't allow it to happen. It was as simple as that.

But another man kissing Winter? Hell and blue blazes!

Robert left the front of the house and wandered toward the rear on the off chance Winter was on the patio. His mother, according to her early-morning telephone call, was going off to pretend she was visiting Dodge City, or some such insane thing. And, no, Mother, thank you, but he didn't wish to tag along.

He'd driven to Winter's to . . . Robert shook his head. He really didn't know why he was there. But now that he was, where was Winter?

Suddenly, the sound of a woman singing floated over the stillness of the desert, filling the air with a rich, velvety resonance. Robert stopped dead in his tracks, hardly breathing as he listened intently to the spellbinding voice.

"I cry in the darkness . . . my tears fall like rain . . . there's no place to run to . . . from heartbreak and pain."

He stepped cautiously forward, his heart beating hard.

"My lover has left me . . . with no word of good-bye . . . my spirit is shattered . . . as alone I now cry."

He reached the gate to the patio and looked over it. Winter was sitting in a chair shaded by the umbrella. She was weaving a basket from material she'd placed on the table, her fingers flying with the skill of someone who had mastered the craft. And she was singing.

"The rising sun . . . the rising sun."

Robert knew, as he stared at her, why she had seemed familiar. He knew where he had seen her before.

"It brings me a new day . . . I'm safe from the night . . . it warms me, it soothes me . . . I need not take flight . . . the rising sun."

His throat tightened with a foreign ache as her beautiful voice stroked him, filled him. The sad lyrics seemed to touch his very soul.

"I won't love another . . . I won't give my heart . . . for here I will stay . . . never to part . . . from the rising sun . . . the rising sun . . . my rising sun."

She stopped singing, but continued to hum the melody of the poignant song. Robert took a steadying breath before he attempted to speak.

"You're Bright Winter Star," he said, his voice rough. "You're the famous singer Bright Winter Star."

Winter gasped and jumped to her feet, the basket falling unnoticed to the ground. Despite her dark skin she was suddenly pale, her eyes wide as she stared at Robert.

"No," she said.

He walked through the gate and crossed the patio to stand in front of her.

"I knew I'd seen you before," he said, "but I couldn't think of where it might have been. Now I know. It was four or five years ago. Bright Winter Star, the Indian princess, was at the top of the charts. You were always seen in public wearing a white buckskin dress with beads. The Indian princess . . . Yes."

"Robert," Winter said, her voice weak, "don't. Please don't."

"That song you just sang was written by you, and was the last record you made before you . . . Lord, Winter, I remember it all now. You disappeared. There were endless rumors, speculations, about what had happened to you, where you'd gone. People were talking about it for months. You just seemed to have dropped off the face of the earth. That last song was played everywhere, over and over. You really are the Indian princess. You're Bright Winter Star."

"Stop it," she said, her eyes filling with tears. "I don't want to hear any more. That part of my life is over, that nightmare is ended. I'm Winter Holt, who owns a gift shop in Tucson, Arizona. That's who I am. Are you listening to me? *That's who I am.*"

"Ah, Winter," Robert said, gathering her into his arms.

Even as Winter struggled for control of her emotions, she savored the solid strength of Robert's body and allowed herself the luxury of feeling safe and protected in his embrace. Just by holding her he seemed to push the haunting, painful memories away.

After a minute she eased herself from his arms, then dashed the tears from her cheeks. Lifting her chin, she met his gaze directly.

"So now you know," she said. "It's old news around here. It caused a stir at first, but when I refused to discuss it, just went about the business of opening my store, settling into my house, living my life, people came to accept me for who I am. Just me, Winter Holt. I started over, made a new life for myself. There is no Indian princess. Bright Winter Star doesn't exist."

Robert took one of her hands in his and urged her to sit down in a chair opposite him. He picked up the basket that had fallen, looked at it for a long moment, then set it on the table. He leaned forward, resting his elbows on his knees and lacing his fingers together.

"Talk to me," he said quietly. "Winter, please. What happened? I can see the pain in your eyes. Who hurt you?"

"*I* did." She shook her head. "I don't want to talk about this, Robert."

"Don't shut me out. It's killing me to see your hurt, the sorrow on your face." Why? he wondered. Why was he pressing her, determined to make her share it all, then somehow make her smile again? Hell, he didn't know why. All he knew was that it was important that she realize she wasn't alone. *He* was there now. "Winter, I need to know."

And she needed to tell him, Winter thought. It was suddenly imperative that Robert understood. He had to know who she had been, so he could know who she was now. Why she felt this driving desire to bare her soul to him, she couldn't fathom. But the fact remained that she had to tell him.

"All right, Robert." She drew in a deep breath, then let it out slowly. "I was born and raised in

Flagstaff, then lived at home while I went to Northern Arizona University up there. I majored in business, but my dream, my fantasy, was to sing, to be a famous singer." She sighed.

"There's nothing wrong with that dream. Lord knows you're talented."

"Oh, but I went about it all wrong. I was so naive and immature. I wouldn't listen to my parents, to anyone. I just packed up and went to Los Angeles, determined to be 'discovered.' I got a job as a waitress in a restaurant that had a band and singer perform throughout the evening, and I persuaded the manager to let me sing one song."

Robert nodded, encouraging her to continue.

"The audience liked my voice, my performance. One song led to two . . . then later, after several months, my boss let me have a full hour set each night. I was introduced simply as Winter Holt, with no reference to my being half Indian. I was ecstatic about having the chance to sing, to share songs that I had written. But then . . ."

"Then?" he prompted. "What happened?"

"Word was spreading about me. A man . . . a man named Clifford Foster came to the restaurant to hear me sing. He asked to speak to me after my show, and he said he could make me a star, take me all the way to the top. Lord, that has got to be one of the oldest lines in history, but I fell for it. I could hardly believe my good fortune and like a fool, I signed a contract with him, not fully understanding what all the fancy legalese meant. It wasn't long before I was convinced I was falling in love with Cliff, and he said he loved me. Oh, yes, he loved me, and he was going to guide my career, take care of me. 'Trust me, princess,' he'd say, 'trust me.' And I did. I trusted him with my career and with my love."

Robert's jaw tightened and he felt like hitting something, but his gaze remained fixed on Winter.

"Everything started happening so quickly," she went on, "I could hardly catch my breath. I was suddenly Bright Winter Star, the Indian princess. My trademark was my white buckskin dress. I owned dozens of the exact same dress. The focus was on my Indian heritage. I wasn't allowed to give interviews because I was to create an aura of mystique—the silent Indian, the princess who floated through life singing, but not speaking."

Winter looked up at the sky to regain control of her emotions, to fight back fresh tears. After a moment, she looked at Robert again.

"Nearly two years passed. I made two albums, went on tours, did everything Cliff told me to do. I hated exploiting my heritage, and felt as though I was being disrespectful to my mother, my people. Finally I told Cliff that I didn't want my career slanted that way. He said my contract clearly stated that he was in charge of my 'image.' He sweet-talked me, told me how much he loved me, how he was doing so much for me so I would be rich and famous. More months slipped by, with Bright Winter Star becoming more and more successful. And Winter Holt becoming lost, confused, and terribly unhappy."

"Winter . . ." Robert began, wishing there was some way he could comfort her.

She held up a hand to silence him.

"We were in Chicago for a performance, and guess who showed up at the hotel?" She laughed, a sharp, humorless sound. "Cliff's wife. A wife that for more than two years he had conveniently failed to mention he had."

Robert swore viciously under his breath.

"I was naive not to have suspected, but she, unbelievably, was even more naive. She honestly thought I was just another one of Cliff's clients. She'd left their two children with her mother and flown to Chicago to surprise her beloved Clifford. Because, she said to me, she knew he must miss her as much as she missed him."

"What did the s.o.b. do?"

"He took me aside and said he had to be nice to his wife because she had lots of money and he needed her financial backing. He told me he'd send her packing for home in a couple of days, and we'd be able to pick up where we'd left off. 'Trust me, baby,' he said, but something had snapped inside me. I saw Cliff for what he was. He'd used me, exploited me. He'd never loved me, not for a second. It was a sham, all of it, a stack of lies so big that I was buried beneath them."

Robert muttered another earthy expletive.

"I hardly remember the next few months after Chicago. I was in a haze of pain caused by Cliff's betrayal, by my own shame of making a mockery out of my heritage . . . So many guilts, so many. Then one night in San Francisco, I wrote the song 'The Rising Sun,' the one you just heard. It was my way of gathering enough courage to end the nightmare, to come home, to be an honest and true Chiricahua Apache again. I hid—I actually hid out—at my parents' house until most of the hoopla died down."

"What about Cliff? He had to have been mad as hell."

"Oh, he was. I was making him a very rich man. He hired detectives who found me, and he came to Flagstaff. He said he'd sue me for every penny I had if I didn't come back to him and fulfill the terms of my contract. But *I* told *him* that if he filed suit against me, or ever came near me or any of my family again, I'd have a cozy little chat with his wife."

"Good for you."

"He stormed out, and I've never heard from his since. I was twenty-four years old by then and, believe me, I was no longer immature and naive. No one will ever use me or take advantage of me again. I used the money I'd made singing to start over, fresh, here in Tucson. I traveled to Mexico, New Mexico, Oklahoma, all over the place, to study the crafts of the various Indian tribes. Drawing on the business knowledge I'd learned in college, I carefully, methodically, worked out my plan to open a shop, vowing to make as few mistakes as humanly possible."

Robert nodded.

"When I knew the time was right, I opened my store and named it The Rising Sun. I was telling the truth when I said I called it that as a tribute to the Chiricahua Apaches. But it's more than that. It's the name of the song that I wrote to give me strength to break free of Cliff's hold on me. It's a reminder of where I was, and how far I've come back to being true to myself. The Rising Sun encompasses a multitude of emotions and events. It's fitting that it should be the name connected to my fresh start."

"And the words to the song, Winter?" Robert asked quietly. "What about the words? They say you'll never love again. The reference to the rising sun means, I think, that you've found peace within yourself, are content to live the new life you've created. I suppose some people think it's Indian folklore, or whatever, about communing spiritually with the sun at daybreak."

"I suppose, considering that Bright Winter Star sang the song."

"But what about the rest, Winter? About never loving again? You don't really mean that, do you?"

"Yes."

"Lord, Winter, you're so young, so beautiful, so . . . How old are you? Twenty-six?"

"Twenty-eight. Robert, as I went through the healing process after my fiasco, I built a solid wall around my heart. I don't ever again want to run the risk of loving, of trusting in a man the way I did with Cliff."

"But you were a vulnerable kid. You said yourself that you're no longer immature and naive. You're sentencing yourself to a life alone because of mistakes you made when you were barely more than a child."

"I will never love again."

He sat back in his chair and dragged one restless hand through his hair.

"You're wrong," he said. "You're making yourself pay too heavy a price for past errors in judgment."

She shrugged. "So be it. Robert, my stand on the issue of love isn't that different from yours. You've decided *when* you're going to allow love into your life. If it comes knocking on your emotional door before you're forty, you'll ignore it. If it raps on my door at any time, I'll ignore it. We're not that far apart on our views."

"But . . . Well, hell."

She meant it, Robert realized. She was determined never to love again. And that was wrong. It was obvious from what she had told him that when she loved, she gave of herself totally, unconditionally. She had so much to offer a man, not just in beauty, but in warmth, laughter, sharing. Lord, he'd like to get his hands on that Clifford Foster for five minutes and make him pay for what he'd done to Winter.

Lovely Winter, he mused, who suddenly reminded him of a skittish fawn with her big dark eyes. She was emotionally fragile, yet beneath the surface was the woman of strength who had emerged from the rubble of her involvement with Foster.

"What about children?" he asked, breaking the silence. "With the stand you're taking on not loving again, haven't you also robbed yourself of the chance to be a mother?" He paused. "No, I suppose not. It's not that unusual these days for a single woman to adopt, or choose to have a man's baby, but not marry him."

"I wouldn't do that," she said. "I've thought about it a great deal because I'd like to have a baby more than I can tell you. But I was raised by a loving mother and father, each giving me something special from themselves. I know some wonderful single mothers, but I wouldn't set out intentionally to deprive my child of a father. No, there—there will be no baby."

He shook his head. "This isn't right. Dammit, Winter, you've got to stop and realize what you're doing. You say you built a wall around your heart? Well, for Pete's sake, tear it down. You can't do this to yourself, don't you understand that?"

"No." She reached for the basket she'd been working on and began to weave a narrow strip of material in and out.

"What is that stuff?" Robert asked, momentarily diverted from what he was saying.

"These strips are made from yucca leaves. I get the supplies from the Hopi Indians, even though the Apaches are better known for basket weaving."

He leaned forward for a better look. "You're really fast at doing that."

"I've had years of practice. It's very relaxing to weave a basket, great stress therapy, I suppose you could say. So, I weave, calm down, and end up with a product that is in high demand at my store. I'm sure that as a detail-minded businessman, you can appreciate the efficiency and benefit of the entire system."

"Yes, I can."

"But then I imagine," she went on, not looking at him, "that all aspects of your life, personal and professional, have already been examined and streamlined for efficiency. Have you worked out the details as to how you'll choose your wife when you turn forty?"

He frowned. "Details?"

"Well, heavens, Robert, anyone who is organized to the point of knowing he's going to blow out forty candles on his birthday cake, then say 'I do' in the next breath, surely has a list of must-have qualities for said wife-to-be. Blonde, brunette, redhead? Tall, short, voluptuous, thin? Should adore babies, I would think. What about kittens and puppies, though? Should she like furry little critters, too, or will a slew of kids pass the test?"

"That's enough, Winter," he said, his jaw tightening. "You make me sound like a total jerk."

She plunked the basket onto the table. "Well, you are a jerk. To actually pick an age when you plan to marry—not thirty-nine, not forty-one, but forty, right on the button—is ridiculous."

"No more ridiculous than the idiotic wall you've built around your heart," he said, his voice rising, "because of something you did when you were too young to know better. Now that, Winter Holt, is ridiculous."

"So is your stupid matrimony schedule," she said, matching his glare and his volume. "It's that kind of rigid, stuffed-shirt rationale of yours that is causing your mother so much grief. Why don't you concentrate on chipping away at *your* wall, Robert Stone? You have one, you know, that won't allow you to give an inch, that keeps you on the straight path from here to the end of your life. As far as you're concerned, the wants and needs of anyone other than yourself are unimportant. You're a walking, talking calendar of events that have been written in indelible ink for the rest of your life. And furthermore—"

Robert surged to his feet, gripped her by her upper arms, and hauled her out of her chair. In the following instant, his mouth came down hard on hers, his tongue plummeting into the sweet darkness within. In the next wild beat of their hearts, the kiss gentled, and he wrapped his arms around her, nestling her close to his body.

Winter's gasp of shock at his sudden actions caught in her throat, and eyes that had widened in surprise now drifted closed. Her arms lifted, floating upward to encircle his neck, and she met his tongue with hers, stroking, tasting, savoring.

He hadn't intended to do this, Robert thought hazily, but some of the things Winter had been saying had been unexpectedly difficult to shrug off as untrue, unjust accusations.

Even as his anger had simmered, he'd known he didn't want to fight with her. She had shared with him the very personal anguish of her past, and he cherished the fact that she'd been so open and honest. No, he didn't want to quarrel with Winter—he wanted to kiss her.

And there he was, kissing her.

And the kiss was ecstasy.

His hands roamed restlessly over her back, pressing her closer, closer, his passion heightening as he felt the soft swell of her breasts against his hard chest. He was aware of the heavy weight of her braided hair, and yearned to work it loose until the silken tresses could slide through his fingers like an ebony waterfall.

He drew a quick, ragged breath, then claimed her lips once more, determined that this, what they were sharing, would erase the pain of Winter's past. He wanted her free from dark memories and old ghosts. Free to live, and laugh, and love again.

Free to love *him*.

What? that familiar voice in his mind asked. He had no intention of falling in love, not now. He'd covered all that with Winter last night. He was *not* going to fall in love with this woman.

A soft purr of feminine pleasure whispered from her lips, and all rational thought fled Robert's mind as he filled his senses with Winter.

Oh, Robert, Winter thought dreamily. She hadn't intended to tell him of her past, of the ghosts of shame that haunted her spirit. But now he knew, and for some unknown reason, she was glad he did. And she was glad he was kissing her. Her heart was nearly bursting with the sheer joy of it. She didn't want this kiss to end, not ever.

Somewhere in the far recesses of Robert's mind he knew he was losing control, slipping over the edge of passion's abyss. He ached with desire, burned to mesh his body with Winter's, to unite with her into one entity. Other emotions were intertwined with his raging need, emotions of tenderness, protectiveness . . . and something unnamed that he refused to call love.

But he *must* stop kissing Winter. *Now.*

He lifted his head, then with shaking hands gripped her shoulders and inched her away from his aroused body. She slowly opened her eyes, and he nearly groaned aloud as he saw the desire reflected in those dark pools.

"Oh . . . my," she whispered.

He stepped back. "That about covers it," he said, his voice gritty with passion. "Those kisses were sensational. They were . . . Winter, you're remembering the plan, aren't you?"

"Plan?" She blinked, dispelling the last of the misty haze of desire hovering over her. "Oh! The plan. We don't want to fall in love with each other, and since we're in charge of our emotions, we won't. I'm not falling in love with you, Robert." Was she? Oh, dear heaven, was she? "Don't worry about a thing."

"Well, that's good," he said, nodding. "I'm not falling in love with you, either, so we're in fine shape. We nipped it in the bud, just like I said. I'm doing fine." What he was doing was having a nervous breakdown, he thought. Dear Lord, if this wasn't love, then what was it? No, forget the question, because he didn't have the energy at the moment to deal with the answer. "See what people can do when they set their minds to it?"

"Yes. It's amazing." She turned to the table and began to gather her weaving supplies. "I just realized that I need to do some grocery shopping. I don't mean to be rude by rushing you off, but I must get to the store."

"I'll go with you," Robert heard himself say. To the grocery store? For Pete's sake, Robert Stone didn't get a thrill from going to the grocery store. He *never* went to the grocery store. "I like grocery stores."

She turned to face him, her arms full of supplies. "Why?"

"Oh, well, they're fascinating. And organized. Very organized. It's always a pleasure being surrounded by the results of actions put into motion by an organized mind. You know what I mean?"

She eyed him warily. "Not really."

He didn't know what he meant, either. "Let's go to the grocery store," he said wearily.

They went in Winter's van, and she drove with relaxed expertise. There was still a crispness to the air, as though summer had packed its bags and trundled off to parts unknown to grant access to autumn.

"There certainly are a lot of mountains around here," Robert said, looking out the window.

"Tucson is surrounded on three sides by mountain ranges," Winter said. "The Catalinas, the Rincons, the Tucsons. To the south is Nogales, Sonora, Mexico."

"The desert is rather stark, but I guess it

might grow on a guy. There's a bunch of nasty things out there, though, according to what I've read. You know—scorpions, snakes, coyotes . . . friendly critters like that."

She laughed. "The Apaches who still believe in ghosts think they come at night in the form of owls and coyotes."

"Do you believe in ghosts?"

"Me? Heavens, no. There are many other teachings of the Indians that I respect and admire, though."

"Such as?" he asked, shifting to look at her.

"Well, you've seen pictures of Indian women carrying their babies on their backs strapped to a cradle board. People generally assume it's a way of keeping the baby close but still having one's hands free to work."

"Isn't it?"

"Yes, but it's more than that. The baby is at eye level with adults when it's being carried on the mother's back. Self-esteem, self-worth, is instilled in the child from birth. The fact that the child isn't looking up at adults doesn't diminish respect for older people, it prepares the little ones to learn the wisdom of their elders early on by communicating eye-to-eye. Whenever I speak to a child of any age, I bend down to their height and look directly into their eyes."

Robert nodded slowly. "I like that. It makes sense."

Winter glanced quickly at him, then redirected her attention to the road.

"There's another Indian teaching I thoroughly agree with," she said. "Native Americans highly respect the older people in their families. The elderly are revered, old age being considered a time of prestige. To have lived so long means they have overcome all of life's obstacles, are filled with knowledge and sound judgment, and are in harmony with their spirit."

Robert narrowed his eyes. "I know where you're heading with this, Winter . . . straight to the subject of my mother. We were enjoying ourselves. Why muddy the waters today with a topic that will, without a doubt, lead to a rip-roaring argument? Today—today is ours." He leaned over and stroked her cheek with his thumb. "Just the two of us today, Winter. All right?"

A shiver coursed through her as Robert's thumb glided across her cheek, and her hold on the steering wheel tightened.

"All right, Robert," she said softly, not looking at him. "Today is ours."

Five

Today is ours.

From the moment Winter agreed to Robert's plan and echoed his words, a feeling of lightheartedness swept over them. They both smiled, and the day suddenly stretched before them like the Yellow Brick Road.

As Winter drove farther away from the remote desert area where she lived and into the hustle and bustle of Tucson itself, Robert announced that he was ready for lunch. He was so hungry, in fact, he was close to passing out from lack of food.

Winter laughed and obligingly pulled into the parking lot of a Mexican restaurant. During a meal of shredded beef tacos and cheese crisps, they discussed the merits of a controversial book that was currently on the best-seller list.

The subject of books led to movies, then to

professional football teams, and finally to the prediction of who would be playing in the Super Bowl at the end of the season.

They agreed on absolutely nothing, but due to their oh-let's-just-have-fun attitude, they thoroughly enjoyed the debates, each declaring the other to be totally insane.

After lunch, they wandered in and out of the various stores in the mall where the restaurant was located. The candle shop, Winter said with a moan, would be her undoing, as she adored burning scented candles in various rooms of her house.

Inside the store, Robert glanced around with interest.

"These candles are incredible," he said. "Half of them don't even look like candles. Do you see that arrangement of animals, Winter? They appear to be carved out of wood."

"Aren't they gorgeous?" she said, walking beside him to the display. "The colors, the detail . . . I could never bring myself to light one of these. It would be like destroying a beautiful sculpture. They're really magnificent."

He planted his hands on his knees and leaned over for a closer scrutiny. His gaze was caught by a pair of owls sitting nestled together on a branch, whose flat bottom served as a base. The entire candle was approximately six inches high and seven inches long.

"Incredible," he said. "I'd swear that if I touched those owls, I'd feel the softness of feathers." He straightened and smiled at Winter. "I'm going to buy that piece for you."

"Oh, Robert, thank you, but no. I don't want you to buy me anything."

He held up one hand to silence her. "This is an experiment. You, Miss Half Chiricahua Apache, claim you don't believe that ghosts appear at night in the form of owls and coyotes."

"I *don't* believe it."

"Okay, then we'll put it to the test. We'll set these owls on the mantel in your living room and see if they scare the bejeebers out of you. For all I know, you speak with forked tongue, Madam Chiricahua."

Winter narrowed her eyes in an attempt to appear angry, then burst into laughter.

"You're on, Stone," she said. "You're an idiot, but you're on."

Robert nodded decisively, then carefully lifted the candle from the display and carried it to the counter. Winter was right behind him.

The middle-aged woman behind the counter beamed when Robert placed the owls in front of her.

"Oh, what a perfect choice," she said. She removed the price tag and began to wrap the candle in tissue paper. "Is this for you two? Or is it a gift?"

"It's ours," Robert said. He frowned slightly as the words seemed to echo around him, then shrugged. "Yes, it's ours."

The woman looked at Robert, then at Winter, then back to Robert.

"Excellent," she said, reaching for a box. "These are love owls."

Winter blinked. "Pardon me?"

"They're love owls, dear." The woman placed the tissue-wrapped candle in the box. "You saw how they're side by side on the branch, with no space between them. They're connected, they're one, they represent love. So, they're called love owls."

"Oh," Winter said in a small voice. "That's . . . interesting."

"Isn't it, though?" Robert said, chuckling. "Very, *very* interesting."

Winter shot him a glare, then walked away, pretending to look at other candles while Robert paid the woman.

Love owls, Winter repeated, silently. Love owls? She wasn't superstitious, and yet the entire essence of herself as a woman, both the white and Apache sides of her, was quivering with a strange unease at the thought of a pair of love owls sitting on her mantel.

Love owls purchased with Robert Stone.

Love owls that would, no doubt, be put in place by Robert Stone, while she stood next to him.

Love owls who, nestled as close together as they were, with no space between them, were a symbol of strong, unbeatable love in its purest form.

Two love owls. One was Robert, and one was Winter . . .

Oh, for heaven's sake, Winter thought, shaking her head. She was going off on some unsettling romantic tangent over a candle. A person lit a candle, then watched it melt, enjoying its beauty while it lasted.

But as she turned and saw Robert take the bag from the woman, Winter knew with a rather frightening intensity that she would never set a lighted match to the wicks of the love owls.

"All set," he said, walking over to her.

She forced a smile that she hoped appeared genuine. "Okay. Do you realize how late it is? We, sir, had best get to the grocery store."

He bowed. "I'm at your command, ma'am. Lead on."

After locking the bag containing the boxed candle in the van, they entered the large grocery store at the end of the mall. Winter took a list from her purse, Robert pushed the cart, and they started off. Robert's mind wandered as Winter concentrated on the list and the items on the well-stocked shelves.

Love owls, he thought. Holy hell, he'd bought a pair of love owls. And he was going to put them on Winter's mantel, in her home, while she stood right next to him as though they were performing a ceremony.

Well, so what? he asked himself. He'd bought the wax owls out of a sense of fun, befitting the mood that had existed between Winter and him. She had a refreshingly relaxed attitude about her mixed heritage, and he respected and admired her ability to gather to her the wisdom of both of her worlds.

He, too, was comfortable with her dual nationalities, and had purchased the owls as a way to challenge her to prove to him that she hadn't fallen prey to Apache superstition.

And what happened? The candle turned out to be a pair of love owls, representing two people committed to each other forever. Two people forsaking all others. Two people standing side by side during the good times and bad. Woman and man, wife and husband, Winter and Robert . . .

Shut up, Stone, he told himself. He was going to tattoo the message "Think Forty" on his brain. He had places to go, things to do, people to see, money to make. He didn't have time to devote to a wife now. *He would not fall in love with Winter Holt.*

The groceries purchased and the sacks loaded into the van, Winter drove toward home. Silence prevailed for the first several miles.

"It was a lovely day, Robert," she said at last. "I'm—I'm glad you decided to join me."

He looked over at her. "I enjoyed it, too, *and* your company."

She stopped at a red light and her glance fell on the bag from the candle shop that sat between them on the seat. She lifted her eyes to find Robert still looking at her.

"Thank you for the gift," she said softly.

"You're welcome."

Their eyes held until a loud blare of the horn from the car behind them caused Winter to jump. Only then did she realize the light had turned green. She pressed on the gas pedal.

Again silence fell within the van. They both stared straight ahead. They both were acutely aware of the proximity of the other. And they both attempted and failed to ignore the presence of the bag containing the love owls, which seemed to be growing bigger, demanding attention—and acknowledgment of what they represented.

With an inward sigh of relief, Winter at last pulled up next to her house and turned off the ignition.

"Well, here we are," she said, striving for a cheerful tone to her voice. "Home sweet home."

They got out of the van, then turned to meet each other's gaze across the expanse of the seat. Neither reached for, nor looked at, the bag between them.

"You take it," Robert said finally. "I'll bring in the groceries."

As he closed the door and turned to slide back the side panel on the van, Winter reached tentatively for the bag. She hesitated, her fingers hovering over the paper.

For crying out loud, she thought, this is absurd. She was acting as though she were about to touch a live entity that might gobble her up, or cast a spell over her. Really absurd.

She snatched the bag off the seat and marched toward the house. Robert followed, his arms wrapped around three grocery sacks.

When they entered the house, Robert walked on to the kitchen as Winter stopped to place her purse on a chair. She stared at the bag for a long moment before gingerly setting it next to her purse. Abruptly, she spun around and strode into the kitchen.

By sheer force of will, Winter pushed aside the

image of the love owls waiting to be tended to. As Robert unloaded the sacks, she placed the items in their proper places. All the while, she chattered nervously like a magpie.

"Would you like to hear more Indian legends, Robert?" she asked. "Some are fascinating."

"Sure," he said, taking a can of soup from the sack. "Cream of broccoli. That sounds gross. Cream of broccoli *soup*?"

"It's quite tasty. Anyway, legend has it that Ussen, also known as Life Giver and Sky God, sometimes called God of the Sky, created the universe. He created White Painted Woman, also called Earth Mother and Mother of the Apaches."

"There certainly are a lot of aliases there."

"I think the legends probably got changed a tad through the generations. Now then, White Painted Woman had two sons. One was fathered by Lightning, and named Child of the Water. He created the Chiricahua Apaches. Her other son was fathered by Sun, and named Killer of Enemies. He created the white man."

"White Painted Woman was a busy lady," Robert said, chuckling. "Her boys sure set up a potentially messy situation too. A little planned parenthood would have saved a lot of lives way back when."

Winter laughed. "That's a very modern analysis of a very old legend. History speaks the truth, though. Mistakes were made on both sides during the clash between the red man and white. It's easy to stand in judgment now, but at

the time each group of people felt they were doing the right thing. The way it was is . . . well, simply the way it was."

Robert stood with a bottle of catsup in his hand and looked at Winter, a frown knitting his brows together.

"Listen to yourself for a minute," he said. "You're forgiving a multitude of sins of a great many people, on the theory that human beings make honest mistakes. Yet you won't give yourself the same understanding. You're allowing a mistake in judgment made years ago to dictate your entire future. Can't you see the contradiction within yourself?"

"I—I never thought about it like that," she said, turning to face him.

"But it's true, don't you see? You could have a chip on your shoulder a block long about the way the Native Americans were treated in the early west. Or you could go the other route, and be angry as hell because your Indian ancestors massacred so many white people, some of whom might be on your family tree. But instead, you're open-minded, forgiving, recognizing the human frailties in both groups. Winter, don't you like yourself enough, respect yourself enough as a woman who has a successful business and a lovely home, who has accomplished a great deal, to forgive and understand the lack of judgment shown in your actions years ago?"

"Well, yes, I am very proud of The Rising Sun and the reputation it has for carrying only the finest products made by Native Americans. I worked very hard for that, but . . . I . . ." She crossed her arms over her middle, wrapping her hands around her elbows. "Dammit, Robert, since when do you have a degree in psychology? You're confusing me, spouting off like that, like a fancy philosopher."

"I'm not a psychologist, nor a philosopher," he said quietly. He set the catsup on the table and started toward her. "I'm just a man who sees a beautiful, warm, giving woman sentencing herself to a life of loneliness."

Winter dropped her arms to her sides and moved backward as Robert continued his slow advance toward her. Her heart beat frantically as she met his gaze, the intense look in his blue eyes seeming to steal the breath from her body.

"You have a wall, too, Robert," she said, still retreating. "I've said that before. Your wall keeps you from straying off the course you've outlined for your life." She thudded against the refrigerator and pressed her palms flat on the gleaming door.

Robert closed the distance between them and stood directly in front of her, his gaze locked on hers. He planted a hand on either side of her head and leaned closer, until his body was only inches from hers and he'd trapped her in place.

"But you're chipping away at my wall, aren't you, Winter?" he said, his voice very low. "You're tearing it down a little at a time with every smile, every laugh, every time you look at me with those great big fawn eyes of yours."

"No, I'm not doing anything like that," she

said, her voice, her whole body, trembling. "I'm . . . No . . . I'm really not . . ."

"Chip . . ." He lowered his head toward hers. ". . . by . . ." He outlined her lips with the tip of his tongue. ". . . chip."

His mouth melted over hers, his tongue parting her lips. Winter's hands moved from the refrigerator door to press against Robert's chest, then slid slowly upward as she savored the feel of the muscles beneath her palms. She finally encircled his neck with her arms, her finger inching into his thick hair and urging his mouth harder onto hers. Her lashes drifted down as she filled her senses with Robert.

Robert closed the gap of inches between his body and Winter's, and nearly groaned aloud as his heavy arousal met her womanly softness. The kiss intensified as fiery desire flared within him. He drank of Winter's sweetness like a thirsty man, and when she kissed him back just as greedily, he knew her need matched his own. He gloried in that.

He wanted her. She wanted him.

They would be one.

They would not, he realized hazily, have sex. They would make love. And that was how it should be, the only way it *could* be.

Because he was in love with Winter Holt.

He raised his head, drawing in a sharp breath as he stared at her. She opened her eyes and met his gaze, clearly revealing her desire.

Robert waited for anger to sweep through him

like a tidal wave, overwhelming him. Anger at love for coming at the wrong time and pulling him off course, forcing him to deviate from the well-thought-out master plan for his life.

He waited for the fear born of the realization that he had lost control of his emotions, his heart, maybe even his very soul. That control was now held by the woman standing before him, and he was left stripped bare, vulnerable.

His muscles tensed as he awaited the staggering onslaught of those anticipated emotions.

They didn't come.

He stared at Winter, and instead of anger or fear, joy filled him. He had found her, he loved her, and she would, somehow, be his for all time.

One word whispered from his lips.

"Para-ah-dee-ah-tran."

Contented, Winter echoed silently. Yes. Mingling with the desire still pulsing within her was a sense of peace, of contentment. Because Robert Stone was there.

She'd been so certain she had all she required in her life. Admittedly she'd yearned at times for a child, and for a special man who would be her partner forever. But she'd never lingered long on those thoughts. It would have been futile, dangerous even, and she'd always quickly retreated behind her protective wall.

But then . . . Robert Stone.

Each time he touched her, kissed her, her heart sang with happiness and the wall was momentarily forgotten.

No, Winter, she told herself. She mustn't do this. She couldn't bear the pain of heartbreak, not again. Robert's insistence that she bury her mistakes of the past, forget them, confused her and caused her to question the decisions she'd made.

She had to gather all of her inner strength to resist her ever-growing attraction to Robert, as well as the fierce desire that swept through her like the flames of a brushfire.

"Robert," she said, hoping her voice was steady, "the ice cream is melting."

"What?"

"There's ice cream in one of the grocery sacks, and it must be melting by now."

"Oh." He straightened, freeing her from the cage made by his arms and body. "Well, we'd better tend to it, right? Right." He whirled around and walked back to the table, quickly removing the remaining items in the sacks. "Here it is."

As he returned to her to place the ice cream in the freezer, a chuckle rumbled in his chest.

He was in love for the first and only time in his life, and the first thing he had discussed with the woman of his heart after discovering he loved her was that her ice cream was melting. This was not the stuff from which romantic movies were made.

But he liked the rather bizarre scenario. It was unique, it belonged to him and to Winter, and they could smile about it when they were old and gray and their bones creaked.

"Did I miss something?" she asked. "You're smiling as though you have a secret."

He closed the freezer door.

Oh, he had a secret, all right, he thought, but this was not the time to share it. Winter was too skittish, too frightened, too haunted by the ghosts of her past, to welcome the announcement that he was in love with her. He'd have to be patient.

"I was thinking about my mother," he said. "I wonder if she'll buy herself a ten-gallon cowboy hat while she's in Old Tucson. I hope she's enjoying the outing. It's certainly different from anything she's done before."

Winter frowned and cocked her head to one side. "You're pleased that Bessie is having a new experience, an adventure of sorts? That . . . well, that just doesn't sound like you, Robert."

"It doesn't?" He raised his eyebrows in an expression of pure innocence.

"No," she said, eyeing him closely, "it certainly doesn't."

She put several cans of fruit and vegetables into a cupboard, shooting him a suspicious look as each was thudded into place. Robert smiled at her pleasantly, as he folded the grocery sacks.

"Done," he said. "We took care of that chore in short order. We're a great team. Don't you think so, Winter?"

She narrowed her eyes. *Now* what was he up to? she wondered. A great team? Like a husband and a wife were "a great team"? No, she was reading too much into what he was saying. She'd made a big deal about his remark concerning Bessie, and he was no doubt just making idle conversation. She had to calm down, stop overreacting.

"It'll be dinnertime soon," she said. "I wonder when Bessie is due back."

"Why don't we go out to eat? My mother can fix herself something whenever she gets here. Now that she's discovered she enjoys cooking, there's no reason to be concerned about her not having a proper meal. Those enchiladas she fixed were very tasty. She's doing extremely well in her culinary efforts, considering she never cooked before in her life."

"Robert," Winter said, folding her arms across her chest, "did you have a brain transplant in the last few minutes?"

He laughed. "That's funny. I swear, Winter, you really do have a terrific sense of humor. A brain transplant." He chuckled and shook his head. "That's great."

"Robert . . ."

"Well, it's time to pick a spot for the new candle, don't you think? Where do you want to put the owls? The *love* owls."

"On—on the mantel in the living room."

"Perfect," he said, starting toward the swinging door. "That's exactly the spot I mentioned when we were in the store." He stopped and looked at her over his shoulder. "Are you coming?"

"Yes, of course."

In the living room, as Robert began to unearth the owls from the bag, the box, and the tissue paper, he decided that love was truly amazing.

Here he was, calmly discussing dinner and candles, when the plan he'd made for his life eons ago had just been royally screwed up. He certainly was adjusting quickly. But love was obviously a powerful force. What he had to hope and pray for was that it was strong enough to break through Winter's protective wall too.

"Okay, here we go," he said, cradling the owls in both hands.

Winter crossed the room and met him in front of the fireplace. She stared at the owls, then met Robert's gaze.

"They really are lovely," she said, and was distressed to hear a thread of breathlessness in her voice. "If it weren't for the wicks on the tops of their heads, no one would suspect they're made of wax. And, no, Robert, I don't believe they'll turn into ghosts when darkness falls."

"They're not eligible to be ghosts."

"What do you mean?"

"They already have an assignment," he said seriously. "These are love owls, Winter. They represent the magic of love between two people. They don't have time to be flitting around as ghosts, scaring people to death. What they're doing is far more important."

She leaned slightly toward him, staring at him as though he'd just told her he'd been an Apache warrior in a former life. "Robert, are you listening to yourself? You've said you hope your mother has a grand time on her outing and enjoys her new adventure. This from a man who has hollered to the hilltops that Bessie Stone is too old for adventures? You praised her cooking, even though yesterday you declared that her learning to cook at this stage of her life is dumb. Now you're coming across like a true-blue romantic, caught up in the whimsical notion of these candle figures actually being assigned the job of love owls so they don't have time to be ghosts."

She shook her head. "This is crazy. *You* are crazy. You stood on my patio and discussed love, not falling in love, as pragmatically as you would a business deal." She paused. "Well? Don't you have something to say?"

"Yes. May I set this on the mantel now? I'm getting cramps in my fingers."

She rolled her eyes heavenward. "Yes, Robert, put the owls on the mantel."

"Right."

He lifted his hands so slowly that Winter held her breath, mesmerized by the impression he was giving that what he held was made of the most delicate, fragile substance known to man. When she felt a sudden pain in her chest, she drew in a deep, much-needed breath of air, though her gaze remained riveted on Robert's hands.

He put the candle in place, then carefully removed his hands. Winter stared at the two birds, as did Robert. Neither spoke, nor moved. The room around them seemed to fade as they became encased in a rosy, sensual mist that encompassed only them and the love owls.

With the eerie mist came the throb of desire, pounding within them, setting their hearts to thundering. At the same moment they shifted their gazes from the candle to each other, and passion pulsed deep inside them. Their eyes sent messages of mutual need, undeniable and irresistible.

Winter's knees began to tremble as she was consumed by sensations more powerful than any she'd felt before. Yet the voice of caution in her mind refused to be stilled, and it urgently whispered warnings of heartbreak to come.

Run, she told herself. She had to escape from the mesmerizing spell that seemed to be holding her in place, unable to move.

Think, her mind demanded. She had to remember the pain loving had brought her in the past. She had to stay behind her protective wall where she was safe. Love might initially be gentle, but it could also be filled with lies, with punishing blows that could smash her heart into a million pieces.

Robert was baffling her with his sudden switches in attitudes, and he was chipping, chipping, chipping away at her wall. He might soon leave her unshielded, vulnerable. And then he would go, walk out of her life. If she succumbed to love she would be left, alone and lonely.

Robert lifted his hands to Winter's shoulders, and his thumbs stroked her neck with tantalizing slowness. His gaze roved over her face, lingering on her lips, then meeting her eyes.

"Winter," he said, his voice husky with passion, "I want you." *I love you.* "I ache for you." *I love you.* "Don't be afraid of me, of what's happening between us. I won't hurt you, I would never hurt you." *Because I love you.*

Unexpected tears filled Winter's eyes, and she tried in vain to blink them away. Two escaped nonetheless, sliding down her cheeks.

"Robert, please. Leave me alone," she said, hardly able to get any words past the tightness in her throat. "Whatever this is between us, I don't want to pursue it. I can't. I just can't."

"Winter . . ."

"No." She stepped back, forcing him to drop his hands. "Why won't you believe me when I say I won't love again? Has that made me a challenge to you, triggered the machismo streak in you and made you determined to have me before you leave Tucson? Then, of course, you'll pick up your scheduled life where it was, before it was so rudely interrupted."

"You've got it all wrong, Winter. You're making me pay for something another man did to you years ago." He held one hand over his heart. "This is me, Robert Stone, and this is now. Oh, Lord, Winter, please give me a chance, give *us* a chance."

"To do what? Have a fling while you're here? A fun little romp in the hay? Only during, of course, the time you have free, when you're not busy attempting to shape up your naughty mother so you can catch a plane out of here. No, thank you, Robert, I'll pass. Casual sex just isn't my style."

"I'm not talking about casual sex!" he yelled.

"Well, what would you call it?" she yelled back.

"Making love! There's a helluva difference between the two, Winter Holt."

"And you're playing word games, Robert Stone. The bottom line would be the same. You're leaving Tucson as quickly as you possibly can. I'm sure you're unaccustomed to hearing this word from a woman, Robert, so listen carefully. It's 'no.' N . . . O . . . no. I haven't any intention of—"

The telephone rang, interrupting Winter's tirade. She strode across the room to one of the end tables and snatched up the receiver of the phone.

"Hello? . . . Yes, this is Winter Holt. . . . Pardon me? . . . Oh, no . . . What? . . . Yes, of course, I'll go immediately. . . . Yes, yes, I'm on my way."

She dropped the receiver into place and looked at Robert, her eyes wide.

"That was the concierge at The Chiricahua Hotel. She just received word that Bessie was taken ill while the group was at Old Tucson. Bessie had given my name and telephone number on the card they fill out when participating in an event sponsored by the hotel and . . . Oh, God, Robert, Bessie is at St. Mary's Hospital. We have to get there right away. I said I'd come as quickly . . ." She started toward the door, grabbing her purse as she went.

"Damn," Robert said, hurrying after her. "What's wrong with my mother? Didn't they say anything else? What does 'taken ill' mean?"

At the front door, she looked up at him. "I

don't know what happened. I don't know anything beyond what I said. Bessie needs us, Robert, and we've got to hurry. Bessie needs us." She opened the door and ran out to her van.

Six

The nurse at the hospital admittance desk was kind and sympathetic and spoke in a gentle, understanding manner. Her pleasant demeanor, however, did not erase the fact that the information she had on Bessie Stone was not encouraging.

"Mrs. Stone," she said in her calm voice, "was brought in about an hour ago, and she was suffering from chest pains. She did not," the nurse added quickly when both Winter and Robert paled, "seem to be in extreme pain. A physician is examining her now."

Winter saw the muscle pulsing in Robert's tightly clenched jaw, and when he opened his mouth to deliver what she figured would be a harsh demand that he be taken to his mother *now*, she placed one hand on his arm.

"Robert, all we can do is wait. Let's sit in those

chairs over there. They'll tell us what's happening as soon as they can."

"Of course we will," the nurse said. She picked up a clipboard. "We need this form filled out for Mrs. Stone, please."

"Certainly," Winter said. She took the clipboard with her free hand. "Come on, Robert."

"Now look—" he started.

"Robert," Winter said, tightening her grip on his arm, "come . . . on."

He looked at her, at the nurse, then back to her. With a frustrated shake of his head, he strode to the carpeted waiting area and slouched down onto one of the plastic chairs.

Winter followed slowly. She sat down next to him and gave him the clipboard. He scowled as he filled in the form, then returned it to the smiling nurse. When he resumed his seat next to Winter, his expression was still stormy.

"What's taking so long?" he asked gruffly. "They must have *something* they can tell us."

Winter glanced around the empty room. "There may have been other people who needed attention. Emergency rooms are operated on a triage system, not by order of arrival. We have no idea how long the doctor has actually been with Bessie."

"Is that supposed to cheer me up? Hell, I don't even know what happened, although 'chest pains,' even if they weren't 'extreme,' isn't too damn encouraging."

"I realize that, Robert," Winter said quietly. "I'm very concerned about Bessie too. We have to be patient, because we have no other choice. All we can do is wait."

He dragged his hands down his face, then inhaled deeply.

"Okay," he said. "I'm getting it together. I'm under control." He shook his head. "That form I filled out asked if my mother was on any medication. I don't know. It asked if she was presently being treated by a doctor for a particular ailment. I don't know. It asked for the name and address of her current physician. Hell, Winter, I don't know. Great son, huh?"

"Quit being so hard on yourself. It's been many years since you've lived under the same roof with Bessie. You can't be expected to know those kinds of details about her."

"Oh?" He looked at her. "Do you know the name of your parents' physician? What medication they're on, if any? The general state of their health?"

"Well, yes, but . . ."

"I rest my case. I'm a lousy son."

Winter leaned back in her chair and crossed her arms. "Fine," she said, looking straight ahead. "You're a lousy son."

"Thanks a lot."

She sat up and turned to him. "For heaven's sake, Robert, would you just stop it? Your concern is showing itself in the form of anger. You can dump on me all you want to, but I'll sock you in the eye if you yell at Bessie when you see her."

"I'm sorry. You're right. I guess part of my problem is that this is bringing back painful memories of when my father died. I was in his office going over some details with him regarding a complicated merger we were working on. All of a sudden he got a strange look on his face, sort of confused, or surprised. He said, 'Bobby, please get your mother. I'm going to need my Bessie.' Then he just crumbled. He'd had a massive stroke and never regained consciousness. God, it was a nightmare."

"Oh, Robert," Winter said softly, "it must have been horrible for you and Bessie."

"I didn't really have time to comfort her much. I turned her over to her friends and our relatives. Large corporations can't be put on hold while a son grieves for his father. I was thrust into the role of president, and hundreds of people were counting on me. I left for Paris right after the funeral. I kept in constant touch with my mother by telephone, and she seemed to be adjusting. I flew home several times in the next months, and during my last trip to New York, she told me she was planning a visit to the southwest with two of her friends."

"And weeks later you received her letter saying she was staying on here with me."

He nodded. "The people I left in charge are certainly competent. I've checked in with them a few times and everything is running smoothly. But . . ."

"But what?"

"I was angry at my mother, Winter, because I'd decided that she was coping beautifully with the death of my father. I'd mentally crossed her off the list of problems I had to tend to. She messed up my program with her grand spurt of independence and defiance."

"I understand."

"Do you? What do you understand? The same things I do? The fact that I'm a selfish, self-centered jerk, who forgot somewhere along the line that Bessie Stone is a person, a human being with hopes and dreams? She's not a robot designed to perform in a certain manner that's most convenient for me. She obviously did exactly that for my father all those years, and I can sure as hell see that she has no intention of allowing *me* to push her buttons the rest of her life. No wonder you were cheering her on. She was going after things she had every right to have. I listened to what she said when I arrived here, Winter, but I didn't *hear* what she was saying."

Winter placed one hand on his knee. "It's not too late, Robert. You can tell Bessie all the things you've just told me. She'll realize how much you've . . . well, grown. You'll be giving her a precious gift—the essence of who she is. She'll know that you respect her as a person, someone who is capable of thinking for herself. No, it's not too late."

"How do I know that?" he asked, pain shadowing his eyes. "She could have had a heart attack! Dammit, Winter, what if it *is* too late for my mother to pursue new adventures?"

"Robert, please calm down. I realize this waiting, this not being told anything about Bessie's condition, is very difficult, but you're allowing your imagination to run wild, to create the worst scenarios possible. Where's your sense of command, you're I'm-in-charge-here personality? Robert Stone, you're losing it. Now get a grip on yourself."

He stood up and walked over to one of the windows, bracing his hands high on the frame as he stared out. Darkness had fallen, and the amber streetlights in the hospital parking lot cast an eerie glow.

Oh, he'd lost it, all right, he thought. From the moment he'd stepped from that airplane onto Arizona soil, he'd begun to lose control of his well-ordered, totally organized life. Lord, he'd even fallen in love—heart, mind, body, and soul.

Now he was questioning his relationship with his attitude toward his own mother. He was besieged by guilt as he faced the realization that he'd shoved Bessie Stone into a slot labeled "mother," expected her to behave in the manner she always had, and then, for the majority of the time, actually dismissed her from his thoughts.

Hell, he thought, it was as though he didn't know who he was anymore. Since meeting Winter Holt, his life had been turned upside down and inside out.

If given the chance, he wondered, would he push back the clock? Would he choose to be the man he'd always been before he'd succumbed to Winter's spell? Would he prefer to proceed on course, never having kissed or touched or lost his heart to Winter?

He didn't know what he wanted or who he was. He didn't know *anything*.

"Miss Holt? Mr. Stone?" a deep voice said.

Robert whirled around as Winter got to her feet. A tall, thin man in his mid-thirties, wearing dark slacks and a white smock, crossed the room. He smiled as he extended his hand to Winter.

"I'm Dr. Pierce," he said. He shook Winter's hand, then Robert's.

"How's my mother?" Robert asked.

"Well, first of all," Dr. Pierce said, "let me say that she's a lovely, absolutely delightful lady. Her zest for life, her enthusiasm, is very refreshing." He ran one hand over the back of his neck. "However, I'm afraid that her youthful frame of mind doesn't quite match up with the condition of her body. Her heart, to be specific."

Winter felt an icy fear twist in her stomach. Without realizing she had done so, she reached for Robert's hand and gripped it. His strong fingers tightened around hers.

"What is . . ." Robert started, then cleared his throat. "What is wrong with my mother's heart?"

"It's sending out warning signals," the doctor said, "that Mrs. Stone is headed for trouble. She had a very mild—and I stress *mild*—heart attack today. I called in a heart specialist to verify what I saw on the EKG. He agreed with my conclusions."

"Which are?" Robert asked.

"Mrs. Stone is very fortunate that her heart decided to demand attention before any real damage was done. That puts her in charge of the situation, able to keep one step ahead of things. However, she and I don't see eye-to-eye on a few issues."

"What do you mean?" Winter asked.

"I've talked with Mrs. Stone at some length," Dr. Pierce said. "Because I don't have her medical history available to me, I had to gather my facts from her. This is the first hint of heart problems she's had. She told me that she's visiting here, presently staying with you, Miss Holt. She outlined her plans to rent a home in Tucson for the winter, attend lectures here, concerts, go on side trips that appeal to her, even fly to New York when the mood struck. That's where we crossed swords."

"You don't approve?" Robert asked.

"I do, but I don't. I hate the idea of dampening Mrs. Stone's desire to take on 'new adventures,' to quote her. But I have to be cautious. I'm not saying she won't be able to do as she wishes in the future, but first things first. It's my recommendation, Mr. Stone, that your mother return to New York and place herself in the care of the physician she says she's had for many years. He can run further tests, regulate her diet, set up a program of exercise, and generally keep close tabs on her, for a while at least."

"I see," Robert said gravely.

"That doctor *knows* Bessie Stone, and is in a far better position than anyone here to set things to rights. Down the road, Mrs. Stone might very well be able to return to Tucson and carry out her plans, within reason. But for now, I feel she should go home."

"No," Winter said. "Oh, Dr. Pierce, couldn't

you tell how important it is to Bessie to be here? We have some of the finest heart specialists in the country in Tucson. Why can't she proceed as though she were a resident seeking proper medical attention? Insisting that she return to New York will have far-reaching effects, that extend beyond the miles involved. I'm talking about Bessie's morale, her wonderful determination, her . . .
No, there has to be a solution other than shipping her east for—for repairs."

"Winter," Robert said, releasing her hand, "I'm sure the doctor knows what's in my mother's best interests."

"And *your* best interests, Robert?" Winter asked, turning on him. "What happened to your deep, moving concern that it might to be too late for Bessie to go after what she has the right to have? This is very convenient for you, isn't it? You can dump Bessie back in New York City like you originally planned and go blissfully on your way. But now you don't have to be the bad guy. It was doctor's orders, Mother dear, you can say, and that's the breaks, Toots."

"Now look, Winter—"

"Excuse me, folks," Dr. Pierce said, smiling slightly, "but we have enough to do around here without a double murder in the waiting room. Could we calm down and discuss this rationally?"

Winter's cheeks flushed red with embarrassment. "Yes, of course," she murmured. "I'm very sorry."

"I really don't see where there's anything to discuss," Robert said.

Winter's embarrassment evaporated. "Robert Stone, shut up."

"Whoa," Dr. Pierce said, raising one hand. "May I make a point? I gave you both, as well as Mrs. Stone, my opinion and recommendations. What you two seem to be forgetting is that Mrs. Stone is of sound mind. She's perfectly capable of examining the facts and reaching her own decision."

"In other words," Winter said, "we should butt out."

"Oh, I'm sure you both have every intention of voicing your opinions," Dr. Pierce said. "However, the bottom line is that Bessie Stone will no doubt do as she darn well pleases."

"Great," Robert muttered.

"May we take her home now?" Winter asked.

"No. I'm keeping her overnight for observation. It probably isn't necessary, but I prefer to play things like this very close to the cuff. She's been taken to room two-eleven. You can see her for a few minutes, then be on your way. I'd like her to get a solid night's sleep."

"All right," Winter said.

"And no squabbling while you're with her," the doctor added. "Don't bring up the subject of her leaving Tucson or staying on. Understand?"

"Yes," Winter and Robert said in unison.

"I swear, I'm going to make a great father someday," the doctor said. "Well, good night, folks."

"Good night," Winter said.

"And thank you," Robert added.

As Dr. Pierce left the waiting area, a strained

silence fell between Winter and Robert. They each picked a spot on a far wall and stared at it as though it were the most fascinating thing they had ever seen. Seconds ticked slowly by.

"Well," Robert said finally. "I . . . uh, guess we should go upstairs now."

"Yes."

They turned their heads at the exact same time, and their eyes met.

"Do you feel as though you're just had your hand slapped?" Robert asked, a small smile growing on his face.

"More like I've had my bottom paddled," Winter said, smiling too. "I trust Dr. Pierce, though. He seems very competent." Her smile faded. "We did sound like children quarreling over something we both want, some sort of prize. Bessie is a person. I apologize for my behavior, Robert, and for the things I said. I know you love your mother and want what's best for her. I should step out of the picture and keep my mouth shut, but I don't seem capable of doing that. Bessie has become very important, very special, to me."

He nodded. "I realize that, Winter. I'm not questioning your sincerity in wanting to see my mother do whatever will make her happy. As her friend, that's your top priority. But I'm her son, and my responsibilities are more complex. Let's go say good night to her, shall we?"

"Yes."

He brushed his lips over hers, then circled her shoulders with one arm as they left the waiting area in search of the elevator. He kept Winter tucked close to his side, and she voiced no objection.

It felt so right, she mused, being next to Robert like this. She could feel the strength in his body, the heat that emanated from him and wove into her. They fit together like two peas in a pod—or two owls on a branch.

Oh, no, you don't, Winter told herself. She was not going to dwell on those love owls. They were candles, nothing more. Just a cleverly crafted object made out of wax.

On the second floor, they found room two-eleven. Robert knocked lightly on the closed door.

"Come in," a muffled voice called.

They entered the private room to find Bessie propped against the pillows on the bed, wearing a baggy hospital gown with tiny, light green stripes against an off-white background. She appeared pale, but smiled brightly.

"Hello, Trouble," Robert said, and kissed his mother on the cheek.

"Hell, darlings," Bessie said. "I'm so sorry for all this fuss. There's no reason for me to spend the night here, but that Dr. Pierce is a determined young man. I think he's cute as a button too."

"We can only stay a moment," Winter said. "Dr. Pierce laid down the law to us, as well."

Bessie's smile disappeared, and she sighed. "Bobby, I suppose what happened to me today will give you a new supply of ammunition to use against me."

"No ammunition tonight," Winter said. "Dr.

Pierce forbids it." She leaned over and kissed Bessie on the cheek. "I'm so very glad that you're all right. Have a good night's sleep and we'll see you tomorrow."

"Call me when you've been released, Mother," Robert said, "and I'll come pick you up."

Bessie nodded. "Yes."

"Hey," Robert said, "don't look so gloomy. No one likes to be in the hospital, but it's only overnight."

"It isn't that, dear. Everyone here has been very nice. It's the situation itself that has me distressed. Oh, I don't know. It's as though I'm being told I was acting like a foolish old woman, with my grand plans for new adventures and blissful independence."

"Bessie . . ." Winter started.

"Perhaps," Bessie went on, as though Winter hadn't spoken, "you have the right approach to life, Bobby, by mapping it all out, then sticking to the plan. Heaven knows your father accomplished everything he set out to do by implementing that theory. I tried to make major changes at this late stage in my life, and look what happened." She clasped her hands tightly in her lap and stared down at her entwined fingers. "I feel rather defeated, I guess. I argued with Dr. Pierce about returning to New York, but since then I've been sitting here alone, thinking and thinking, and . . . Oh, dear." Two tears slid down her cheeks.

"Mother," Robert said gently, covering her hands with his, "don't do this, not tonight. You're exhausted, and you've had what must have been a very frightening experience. We'll leave now and let you get some rest."

Bessie slipped her hands free and dashed the tears from her cheeks. "Yes, I'm very tired. But do listen to me for one more minute. I just want to say that I must consider the fact that I may have been wrong about a few things. *I* decided my husband's life was too rigid. *I* decided that your doing the same, Bobby, was also wrong. *I* decided that Winter's stand on never wishing to marry was nonsense, because she'd be such a wonderful wife and mother."

Bessie sighed. "But who am I to stand in judgment? I can't even seem to make changes in my own life, let alone be able to determine what is best for others. I just feel so . . ."

"Now, now, what's all this?" a voice said.

Winter and Robert turned to see an enormous nurse advancing toward them. She carried a small tray with a tiny pleated paper cup on it in one of her large hands.

"Mrs. Stone," the woman said gently, "you're getting yourself in a dither, and Dr. Pierce wouldn't approve. Whatever is upsetting you can be put on hold until tomorrow. I have a pretty pink pill here for you to take so you'll sleep like a baby. These two lovely young people will leave—*now*—and go do whatever it is that lovely young people do together these days. Say good night."

"She's absolutely right, Mother," Robert said. "Come on, Winter, we're out of here."

"Good night, Bessie," Winter said.

"Good night," Bessie said, managing a small smile.

It wasn't until Winter and Robert entered her living room that Winter realized neither of them had spoken since they'd been hustled out of Bessie's room.

"I guess we've both been lost in our own thoughts," she said as she set her purse on a chair. She snapped on several lights, then sank onto the sofa with a sigh. "What Bessie said just before we left keeps bouncing around in my head like Ping-Pong balls."

Robert sat down next to her. "It's strange that you should say that, because it's exactly how I feel. Lord, everything is suddenly so confused and confusing."

She nodded. "Yes."

"Maybe if we talked it through together, we could make some sense out of all of this. What are you thinking, Winter?"

She turned slightly to face him. "It's all jumbled up, Robert. I've been thinking about Bessie's desire to change her life, try new things, explore unknown avenues."

"Go on," he urged.

"But Bessie has linked everything into a tangled chain. Now it's as though we have to reexamine *my* outlook on life, and *your* outlook on life, as well as being concerned as to what's best for Bessie. Am I making any sense?"

"Yes, you are, and we're on the same wavelength. I don't exactly know how all this got mixed together, but you explained it very well. Everything is intertwined all of a sudden." He shifted his gaze to the mantel and stared at the love owls. "My mother is wrong, you know. She wasn't mistaken in believing that my structured, overly scheduled life is absurd, as is your stand on never allowing yourself to love again."

"But . . ."

"No, wait," he said, looking at her again. "Please hear me out. My mother is also wrong in saying that she was foolish to want to make changes in her life. She has every right to do that, and I won't stand in her way."

"Oh, Robert, that's wonderful."

"There's something else you'd better know, Winter." He moved closer to her and took her hands in his. "Winter Holt, I love you. I've fallen in love with you. I'm five years off schedule, but I don't care. To me those love owls on the mantel represent the two of us. I truly love you, Winter."

"No," she whispered. "You mustn't love me, because I don't want . . . But . . . Oh, Robert, don't do this to me, please."

"It's too late," he said, lowering his head toward hers. "I love you, Winter."

"No."

"Yes."

He captured her mouth with his, and she instantly stiffened. No! her mind screamed. But her heart echoed his words.

I love you, Winter. Robert was in love with her. It was glorious, it was . . .

No! Love was nothing more than guaranteed

heartbreak. Love was frightening. Love meant placing one's self in another person's care and standing back to see if that someone would crush it into dust. She didn't want Robert to love her. She didn't want to love Robert Stone.

But she did.

Robert teased her lips open with his tongue, and it seemed her body melted against his. She raised her arms to hold him as her tongue met his, dancing, dueling, heightening passion.

Without breaking the searing kiss, he lifted her onto his lap, his hands roaming across her back, tantalizing her, tempting her.

Winter told herself to think, to realize what she was doing, to run as far from Robert as she could, as quickly as possible.

But as the fire of need consumed her, she could only give way to her senses and abandon the struggle to retain rational thought.

Just one message was clear in her passion-hazed mind. She was in love with Robert Stone.

He'd done it, Robert thought foggily. He'd declared his love aloud, and it felt good, so damn good. Winter, he knew, would war against her growing attraction to him, but he would win. He had to. He was fighting for his life, for his life was Winter.

His hand skimmed along her hip, down to the cuff of her khaki shorts, then on to her bare leg. The feel of her satiny skin made his whole body ache. He loved her. He wanted her.

Winter felt as though she were encased in a lovely, safe cocoon of sensations. She was there with Robert, the man she loved, and no one, not anything, would be granted entry to their haven of ecstasy. No ghosts from the past would be allowed to intrude.

Except, she thought dreamily, the love owls should be with them in their private world. The owls did, indeed, represent the two of them, meshed together so that nothing would separate them. Nothing would destroy the love that kept them as one solid entity.

She hadn't wanted to love, but a force greater than the determination of her mind had touched her spirit and melted the icy barrier around her heart. Robert's wall, too, had been chipped away. He loved her, she loved him, and she wanted to make love with him to declare physically what her inner spirit knew to be true.

"Robert," she whispered, her lips against his, "I want you. I want to make love with you."

A tremor coursed through him as he struggled for control. Winter's softly spoken words had instantly pushed him nearer the point of no return.

"I want you, too, Winter," he said hoarsely, "but I think . . . I think we should wait. Don't you see? I couldn't handle it if you were sorry later, if you regretted what we had done. I need to know you're really aware of what you're doing. I realize that you don't love me, so—"

"I love you."

"What?"

She smiled, a gentle, womanly smile, a smile of inner peace as well as loving desire. She slid her hands from his neck to frame his face, her thumbs slowly stroking his warm skin.

"Robert, I told you that The Rising Sun represented a multitude of emotions within me. It's my strength, my purpose, the essence of who I am. It encompasses my shop, of which I'm very proud. It's a tribute to my people. And it's me, Winter Holt, the woman. I love you, Robert, here in the sphere of my rising sun, my special place that is simply me."

"Winter."

He kissed her deeply, hungrily, then slid one arm beneath her knees and the other around her back. He got to his feet, his precious cargo held tightly to him.

"My bedroom is at the end of the hall," she said, then flicked her tongue over his lips.

Robert started across the room, then stopped, turning to face the mantel. He and Winter stared at the love owls for a long moment before their eyes met again in greater understanding, commitment, and trust.

He turned once more and carried her from the room, neither aware that the eyes of the owls had seemed to shift, watching them go.

Seven

Winter tapped the light switch on the wall as Robert crossed the threshold of her bedroom. Small Indian pottery lamps came to life on the tables on either side of the double bed, casting a soft glow over the room.

The decor was as Robert had expected, a blend of western and Indian done in muted tones of peach, beige, and dusty green. The spread on the bed was Indian-crafted, the furniture was natural oak.

One picture on the wall was a vibrant western sunset melting into a majestic mountain range. On another wall was an oil painting of two women standing together, with the desert and mountains as a backdrop. One woman was in a calico dress and wearing a sunbonnet, her skin fair, the hair that peeked from her bonnet the color of golden wheat. The other woman was an Indian maiden in fawn-colored buckskin, her dark hair falling in braids over her breasts, her skin tawny, her eyes as dark as a starless night.

Each line of the women's bodies spoke of strength and determination. They held their heads high, their backs were straight, and they looked at something in the far distance, leaving it to the viewer to imagine what.

Robert shifted his gaze from the painting to Winter, and smiled at her.

"This room is you. Two cultures meshed perfectly. Oh, Winter, I love you so much."

He dipped his head to claim her mouth, then carried her to the bed and set her on her feet.

"Tell me again," he said, placing one hand on her cheek. "Tell me you love me and that this is what you want."

"I do love you, Robert," she said softly. "And I want to make love with you more than I can find words to say."

He nodded, suddenly unable to speak as emotions closed his throat. By unspoken, mutual agreement, they shed their clothes, then stood naked before each other, offering all that they were.

His hand obviously shaking, Robert reached behind Winter to grasp her thick braid, pulling it forward. He removed the band from the end, then stepped behind her to separate gently the plaited hair.

When her hair was free, he turned her to face him, then sank his fingers into the ebony cascade, watching it glide and fall over her bare breasts like a silken curtain.

"You are," he murmured, "the most exquisite woman I have ever seen."

Winter smiled at him, then slowly traced every inch of Robert's taut body with her gaze. His shoulders were so wide, his arms beautifully proportioned, not overly muscled but obviously powerful. The moist, curly hair on his chest was a shade lighter than that on his head. His legs were long, the muscles in his thighs and calves ropy and well defined.

And his manhood boldly declared his want of her.

"You are exquisite, too, Robert," she said, meeting his heated gaze again. "*Nanta.*"

"What?"

"*Nanta* is Apache for leader, a person of strength both in body and mind, held in high esteem and greatly honored. Oh, Robert, make love to me."

He swept back the blankets to reveal crisp white sheets, then lifted Winter into his arms and laid her in the center of the bed. Stretching out next to her, he rested on one forearm as he drew his fingers through her hair, creating a glorious obsidian fan on the pillow.

Then he lowered his head and kissed her deeply, losing himself in her taste and scent, giving free rein to the passion that consumed him.

Her eyes drifted closed as she savored the sensations curling through her, the heat pulsing low in her body. She welcomed the ache of desire, the heightened awareness of her own femininity.

She murmured a soft protest when his lips left hers, then sighed when she felt them at her breasts, his tongue laving one nipple, before he drew the soft bounty into his mouth. A purr of pleasure whispered from her throat, and she trailed her hands over his broad back, relishing the feel of his hot, smooth skin, his muscles bunching and shifting.

They touched, kissed, explored the mysteries of each other's body and gloried in the discoveries made. They murmured endearments, not fully realizing that the words in their hearts were being spoken aloud. And then they could bear no more.

"Oh, Robert," Winter whispered. "Please. Please."

"Yes, Winter. Oh, yes."

He moved over her, catching his weight on his arms, then kissed her until they were both gasping for much-needed air.

"I love you," he said hoarsely.

"And I love you."

He entered her slowly, watching her face for any sign of pain, but saw only desire reflected there. She wrapped her arms around his glistening back, her legs entwined his powerful thighs, and she urged him on, wanting him, all of him, to consume and fill her.

He thrust deeply within her, and for a moment lay still, stunned by how perfect she felt. Then he began the rocking rhythm that she matched in the next instant. It was beautiful. It was ecstasy. It was a meshing into one entity, bringing them closer than the owls nestled on the branch. They were no longer able to discern where her body ended and his began, as they ebbed and flowed toward the climax they sought.

It came in an explosion of rippling spasms that engulfed each of them only seconds apart. They clung together, calling out each other's name. They hovered there, in passion's heaven, gathering the memories of this most perfect joining.

Slowly, reluctantly, they floated back to reality. Robert rolled onto his back, taking Winter with him. She stretched out on top of his cooling body, her head nestled on his chest. He stroked her hair as they waited for the haze to clear, their heartbeats to return to a normal pace.

"Incredible," he finally said.

"Yes."

"I've just made love for the first time, Winter. What's gone before has been simply sex, physical release. I know that now."

"Yes."

They fell silent again, sated, drifting on the edge of sleep.

"Para-ah-dee-ah-tran," he said quietly. "I am contented."

"Para-ah-dee-ah-tran," she echoed.

"Ah, Winter, it's going to be so fantastic. You can travel with me to the offices I have in Paris, Rome, London, New York. We'll see all the sights, cover every inch of the cities. Then later, when we decide to start a family, we'll pick a place and find a big house with a yard and trees.

I'll organize things differently so I won't have to travel so much. You know, give more responsibilities to my vice presidents so I can be a good father, be right there when our children need me. Upper New York State is beautiful, and I know of some classy houses with lots of grass, and trees, and . . ."

He suddenly realized that Winter's body had stiffened and she'd raised her head to stare at him.

"Robert . . ."

He chuckled. "Forgot something, right? The little matter of officially asking you to marry me. Miss Holt, would you do me the honor of becoming my wife?"

"Robert . . . You're moving too quickly. Can't we slow down a bit?"

"Why? We love each other, Winter." He laughed. "The shock of that fact hit us both like a brick wall, I guess, but we're past the point of being so stunned that we can't think straight. We need to make plans, map out our future." He paused as she shivered. "Are you cold? I hate for you to move because you feel so good, but I'll pull up the blankets."

"All right."

Robert shifted her off him, but kept her close to his side as he drew the sheet and blanket over them.

"You must be starving, Robert," she said. "We never had dinner."

"We'll fix something later. Unless, of course, you want to eat now."

"No, I'm not hungry at all."

"See? That old adage about being able to live on love is true."

"I think," she said, "that the saying is that one *cannot* live on love alone."

"Whatever. Where was I? Oh, yes, we're planning our future."

She sighed. "No, Robert, *you're* planning our future. I have a voice, you know, an opinion."

"Well, of course you do. Tell me what's wrong, if anything, with what I've outlined so far."

She propped a pillow against the headboard and sat up, tucking the sheet under her arms to cover her bare breasts.

"Just about everything is wrong with it," she said, staring straight ahead.

Robert frowned, then pushed his pillow up so he could sit next to her.

"Winter, talk to me. What's wrong with my ideas?"

She turned her head to meet his gaze. "Robert, I live in Tucson, Arizona, on the desert, which I adore, for it brings me a sense of peace. I have a shop that I'm very proud of. I started it from scratch and worked hard, nurturing it into what it is today."

She shook her head, her tousled hair swinging with the motion.

"You're dismissing my home and livelihood as though they're of absolutely no importance. I'm just supposed to chuck all this . . ." She swept one hand through the air, causing the sheet to slip. She quickly yanked it back in place. "You want me to travel with you? And do what while you're conducting business? Sit around like some ornament until you have time for me?"

"Winter . . ."

"You seem to be forgetting," she went on, "that I traveled extensively while I was singing. I gave performances in major cities here *and* in Europe. I lived out of a suitcase, in hotel after hotel, and sometimes I'd actually forget where I was. I can remember searching a room for the hotel stationery so that I would know from the letterhead what city I was in."

"It wouldn't be like that. I sometimes spend weeks, even months, in one place."

"Oh, Robert, you don't understand. Weeks, months, it still isn't permanent. We'd stay in a hotel, or a furnished, rented house. House, Robert, not home. To me, those two words aren't interchangeable. The lifestyle you're describing isn't what I want, or what I need to maintain my inner peace."

"But we'd be together. Doesn't that count for anything?"

"Yes, of course it does, but . . . but it wouldn't be enough. What about my store, what about The Rising Sun?"

"Winter, you're talking about a little shop that sells stuff to tourists, compared with a multimillion dollar corporation. You can't expect me to sit in the middle of this godforsaken desert twiddling my thumbs while you peddle sheep dung pots. Come on, Winter, be reasonable."

With difficulty, she reined in her temper, sparked by his condescending words. "I'm willing to compromise, Robert, but at the moment I don't see where the middle of the road is for us. It's as though you stepped from behind your wall long enough to fall in love with me. But now you want to go scrambling back behind that wall, taking me with you, and map out our entire lives. I'm suppose to leave behind everything that is of significance to me and go blissfully off with you as a starry-eyed bride. I cannot, and will not, do that."

Robert folded his arms over his chest. "Well, this is just great. What do you propose we do? Have one of those ultramodern marriages where the couple lives separately and connects whenever possible? According to a friend of mine who's a psychologist, that sort of arrangement, or any other that is untraditional, is called a 'creative solution.' It's supposed to be a means by which two people who are in love can remain married without either one sacrificing a damn thing. He thought it was terrific, the perfect answer for him and his wife. I, personally, think it stinks."

"Robert, look—"

"No. A wife belongs with her husband. I can remember asking my father if my mother minded being left in New York for such long stretches of time, and he said Bessie was perfectly happy. Well, she obviously wasn't. Her true feelings on the subject have come to light since she's been here. I don't plan to play mind games like my father did. I know, and I'm making it clear, that I want you with me, and you're saying that you won't go."

"I have news for you, Mr. Stone," Winter said tightly. "I'm going to tell you exactly where *you* can go, and what you can do when you get there, if you make one more snide remark about my *little* shop where I *peddle*—peddle? Oh, that's despicable—sheep dung pots. The Rising Sun happens to be very, very important to me and . . . Oh, forget it."

She turned her head so she was no longer looking at him and massaged her now-throbbing temples with her fingertips, being careful that the sheet remained securely tucked across her breasts.

Silence hung over the room like an oppressive weight. Several minutes passed.

"I'm sorry, Winter," Robert finally said. "That was a cheap shot about your store, and I apologize. I was feeling frustrated, but that's not a viable excuse for what I said."

She dropped her hands to her lap, looking at them rather than meeting his gaze.

"Well," she said softly, "this might give you even more insight into how frustrated Bessie felt when she was attempting to change *your* views on an issue that was important to her."

He nodded. "It does. I won't stand in my mother's way if she's still determined to spend the winter here. She can have her medical records sent out. I did listen *and* hear what she said . . . eventually. I'm just hoping you'll do the same for me."

Winter snapped her head around and stared at him. "Me? In my opinion, you have that backward. *You're* not hearing *me*. You think I should be more than happy to walk away from my home, the life I've made for myself here. That isn't going to happen, Robert, but if there's a compromise we can reach, I truly hope we can find it."

"Compromise isn't possible in every area of a relationship," he said in his self-assured businessmen's voice. "It can't always be fifty-fifty. On some issues, one person might have to give one hundred percent, on something else the other person would."

She rolled her eyes in exasperation. "What would you do? Keep a tally to be certain the percentages are staying fairly even? For heaven's sake, Robert, we're talking about our life together, not a business transaction."

"I realize that."

"Do you? Robert, the Apaches have a very clear-cut stand on the relationship between a husband and wife. One person does not dominate the other in any way, because they believe that to do so weakens oneself. Instead, they encourage each other to grow, to become strong, so that their union is an unbeatable force. I admire and respect that philosophy. I've seen it put into effect with loving results in my parents' marriage."

She took a deep breath, then let it out in a weary sigh. "By asking me to give up all that's important to me, Robert, you're trying to dominate me. I can't allow that to happen. I would lose myself, just as I did when I was Bright Winter Star. You fell in love with Winter Holt, but I wouldn't be that woman if I did what you want." She turned to him, feeling fatigue wash over her. "Robert, can't we just put this on hold for tonight? This has been a very full day."

He lifted one hand to her cheek. "Yes, it has, and you're right. I got carried away with making plans for the future. I should have just been savoring the fact that I'm in love for the first time in my life, and loved in kind by the woman of my heart."

"Five years off schedule," she said, smiling. She turned her head to kiss the palm of his hand, then looked at him again. "I do love you, Robert."

"And I love you. We'll find the answers, you'll see."

"Yes."

"In the meantime . . . come here."

She went, eager to escape the turmoil in her mind and to simply rejoice in the love she and Robert had found.

They welcomed the sensuality that spun around them, knowing that while they were encased in its spell, they would share ecstasy that was totally theirs.

They touched, relishing what they'd found before and uncovering new mysteries of each other. Their bodies meshed, their hearts beat nearly as one, and they cried out their love as they were flung over the edge of reality.

Then, with heads resting on the same pillow, they slept.

Several hours later, Winter stirred and opened her eyes. Her lips curved in a gentle smile as she watched Robert sleep. He appeared vulnerable in slumber, unguarded and endearingly younger. He almost looked like a Bobby.

She slipped from the bed and crossed the room to turn out the lights, then made her way back in the darkness. She snuggled close to Robert, savoring his warmth as she waited for sleep to claim her once again.

It didn't come.

Instead, Robert's words as he had planned the course of their life together echoed over and over in her mind. She felt as though she were being crushed by the weight of the implications of what he had said.

She would lose the very essence of herself, she thought dismally. All that was important to her as a person would be gone. She would be nothing more than an extension of Robert, Mrs. Robert Stone, Robert's wife. Winter Holt would disappear as surely as she had when Bright Winter Star came into existence.

She couldn't allow that to happen. She and Robert would have to find a compromise. He had relented on his once-unmovable stand about his mother returning to New York immediately. So, it stood to reason that once he thought things through he'd realize that his initial plan for her and himself was unbalanced, unfair, and unacceptable.

Yes, he'd admit that he'd spoken before he'd properly thought things through.

Wouldn't he?

She'd witnessed Robert at his stubborn worst and knew how strong-willed he could be. What if he gave her an ultimatum that she do it his way, or lose him?

But if she did it his way, she would lose herself.

It all replayed in Winter's mind until she at last fell into a fitful sleep accompanied by disturbing dreams.

Eight

When Winter awoke the next morning, she blinked in shock when she saw that it was nearly ten o'clock. She couldn't remember the last time she'd slept so late.

She blinked again to dispel the last of the fogginess from her mind, and realized she'd awakened to the sound of rain beating on the roof and the sight of a note lying on the empty pillow beside her.

Grabbing the piece of paper as she sat up, she quickly read the message. Robert had written in a bold, sprawling script that he was returning to the hotel to await his mother's telephone call saying she was ready to be picked up at the hospital. He had ended with, 'I love you, Winter. Robert.'

She leaned back against the headboard and sighed.

"I love you, too, Robert," she whispered.

But it was so frightening, she thought. She felt torn in two. A part of her basked in the knowledge that she was in love and was loved, that she'd shared lovemaking with Robert that was more glorious, more exquisite than she'd ever hoped it could be.

She indulged in the luxury of imagining herself as Robert's wife, his other half, until death parted them. She envisioned the baby they would create together, a dark-haired, dark-eyed child who would be a blend of them both.

But, she knew, there was another side to the enchanting scenario. She and Robert were worlds apart in their thinking. Mr. Organized-to-the-Hilt Stone had their life together all mapped out already, detail by detail. That plan did not include Winter's home, nor her pride in and devotion to The Rising Sun.

She shook her head. So many obstacles were in their path, waiting to trip them up. They needed to compromise, but how? Where was the middle ground? Did it even exist, or was she searching for something that was no more than a wistful hope?

She glanced again at the clock, then got up, deciding she preferred not to be found moping in bed when Robert brought Bessie home.

Brought Bessie *home*, her mind echoed, as she opened her closet. No, that wasn't true. She had grown so very fond of Bessie, but their companionship was temporary. Bessie would either choose to return to New York or she'd find her own place to live in Tucson. Bessie was a guest, and would soon move on.

And Robert? she wondered. What about Robert?

Winter quickly showered, then dressed in tan cords and a bright blue sweater. Leaving her hair flowing free down her back, she went in search of her morning coffee.

In the living room, she stopped so abruptly, she staggered slightly. Her eyes were riveted on the love owls on the mantel. She walked slowly toward the fireplace, then tentatively lifted one hand and drew a fingertip over the beautiful, lifelike birds.

Unexpected tears misted her eyes as she continued to stare at this pair that sat so close together on the branch that nothing could ever separate them.

But the owls weren't real, she thought. What they were was an illusion, a clever mastering of an artistic craft that made the birds seem alive. If she set a match to the wicks, the wax would melt until the owls were no more. The love owls would be gone, if not treated with tender care.

Winter turned and walked slowly into the kitchen.

And so it was with love itself, she mused. What was, could be destroyed. What might have been, might never come to be. Love was, as she envisioned it in her mind, strong yet fragile. Nurtured, its strength was unbeatable. Not treated with the proper respect and attention, it could splinter into a million pieces and be lost forever.

She stood at the door to the patio and watched the heavy rain fall as she sipped her coffee. Thunder rumbled and lightning flashed in a jagged line across the dark gray sky.

Desert storms were magnificent, she thought. They were nature at its most basic, raw and powerful, holding nothing back, harsh but honest. Yes, magnificent.

"Hello, hello," a voice called, bringing Winter back from her reverie.

"Bessie," she whispered.

She set her mug of coffee on the counter and hurried into the living room.

"Bessie, I'm so glad you're here," she said, hugging the older woman.

"I thought I was being held for ransom," Bessie said, "but here I am."

"Which is a miracle in itself," Robert said, closing the door behind him. "This weather is horrendous. The roads filled up with water so fast we could hardly get through. It's cold out there too. Wet and cold."

"Ignore him, Winter," Bessie said merrily. "He's grumpy when it rains, always has been, ever since he was a little boy. He doesn't like anything that slows him down, or that he can't control. Now then, due to the fact that Bobby is a man and sadly thinks like one, it never occurred to him that I'd like fresh things to put on today. So, I'm off for a quick bubble bath and clean clothes. I won't be long." With that, she left the room.

Robert quickly walked over to Winter and pulled her into his arms.

"Hello, woman I love," he said, smiling down

at her. "Do you know how beautiful you are when you sleep?"

"I can't say that the subject ever came up," she said, managing a small smile. This was great, she thought. She and Robert couldn't even agree on something as elementary as the weather. "Robert, you didn't say anything to Bessie about us, did you?"

"No, I thought it would be nicer if we told her together. She's going to be thrilled. Winter, if I don't kiss you in the next ten seconds I'm going to pass out from withdrawal symptoms."

She flattened her hands on his chest. "Please, wait, listen to me. I—I don't think we should tell Bessie about us yet."

"Why not?"

"Because we have so many things to work out, problems to solve, decisions to make. I'd rather not say anything to your mother until we have a clearer picture of—of our *mutually* agreed upon plans. Bessie will be so upset if we end . . . up . . . not . . ." Her voice trailed off as she saw Robert's face darken with anger.

He gripped her shoulders. "What in the hell are you saying? Bessie will be upset if we end up not . . . Are we playing fill-in-the-blank? End up not what?"

"Robert, please, let's not argue. All I'm saying is that we have a great many questions that have no answers. I just think it would be best to hold off on any announcement, per se, until we have things worked out."

"Which may, or may not, happen? Is that

what you're implying with your cryptic 'if we end up not . . .' statement? Is it?"

She frowned. "Yes. Robert, the fact that we've realized we love each other doesn't automatically guarantee that we'll be able to reach a compromise that is acceptable to us both in regard to our life together." Oh, Lord, she thought. She was beginning to sound like him.

"The hell it doesn't," he said, his voice rising. "All you have to do is look at those love owls on the mantel. They're together, side by side. They can't be separated without destroying them. That's the answer, Winter. We love each other, we stay *together*—do note the emphasis on the word *together*—and everything is fine."

"It's not that simple!" she exclaimed. She glanced quickly down the hallway toward Bessie's bedroom, then met Robert's eyes again. "Shh. The last thing we need is for Bessie to hear any of this. Robert, please, put your stubborn mode on hold for now. Bessie will be back any minute. Will you agree not to tell her about us for the time being?"

"No." He sighed and dropped his hands to his sides. "All right, yes. But I don't like it."

"We'll talk later when we're alone."

"We'll do a lot of things later when we're alone. And that," he said, framing her face in his hands, "you can take all the way to the bank."

He lowered his head and claimed her mouth in a kiss so searing, it seemed to steal the very breath from Winter's body. She eagerly met the demands of his lips and tongue, savoring the feel of him, and the vivid images in her mind of their lovemaking. A heated mist began to swirl around her as desire awakened deep within her.

Oh, how she loved this man. Robert . . . Robert . . . Rob—

"Well, my stars."

Winter and Robert literally jumped apart, then spun around to face a beaming Bessie.

"This isn't what you're thinking, Bessie," Winter said in a rush of words. She shook her head and pressed one hand to her forehead. "I can't believe I said that."

Bessie walked into the room and sat down in a chair, still smiling with delight. As she looked at them, she laughed.

"You two look like naughty children who've been caught with their hands in the cookie jar. Or playing doctor."

"Cute," Robert muttered.

"I'm so pleased," Bessie went on. "Imagine, the two of you . . . Well, I'm thrilled. I've been so wrapped up in my own concerns that I didn't see what was happening under my old nose. Do you have, shall we say, anything official to announce, any plans you'd care to share with me?"

"No," Winter said quickly and much too loudly. She slid a glance at Robert, and received a glare back. She looked at Bessie again. "We'll keep you posted," she said, striving for a light, cheerful tone of voice. "Yes, certainly. Just like a soap opera. Tune in tomorrow for the next installment of—"

"Winter, for crying out loud," Robert interrupted.

"Sorry," she said, grimacing. "Would anyone like some lunch?"

"No," Robert said.

"No, thank you, dear," Bessie said. "I ate an enormous breakfast at the hospital. It was quite tasty. I wonder if I might ask you two to sit down so I could talk to you?"

They nodded and walked to the sofa, sinking onto it a cushion apart. Bessie took a deep breath, then sat up straighter in her chair.

"Now then," she said, "I slept well last night, due, I suppose, to that pretty pink pill. I awoke very early, which gave me an opportunity to think without being disturbed, and I've reached some rather startling conclusions."

"Oh?" Robert said, raising his eyebrows.

Bessie nodded. "I had become nearly obsessed with exerting my independence since arriving here in Tucson. I saw my life as I'd lived it thus far as being narrow, confining, sheltered, and useless. But this morning I realized that that really wasn't true."

Both Winter and Robert sat forward, curious and intrigued.

"Your father, Bobby, was away more than he was home during the entire course of our marriage. I was in charge of making all the decisions regarding your upbringing, the household staff, the budget. Why, I even put in buy and sell orders to the stockbroker when *I* deemed it prudent to do so. The successful charity events I organized were the result of many hours of hard work, attention to detail, the ability to supervise, et cetera. What I did was as complicated and as efficiently carried out as any assignment for a highly paid CEO would have been."

"Yes," Winter said thoughtfully, "you're absolutely right."

"I did not," Bessie said, "give myself credit where credit was due. I suddenly felt that I had to *do* something with my life before it was too late. I became nearly frantic about staying here, about having adventures, doing things I'd never done before. If I did all that, I thought, I could justify my existence, be able to say, 'See what I've done?' But this morning I said to myself, 'Bessie, you silly old woman, you have no apologies to make to anyone for the space you've taken up on this earth.'"

"Hear! Hear!" Winter said.

"We are, all of us," Bessie went on, "in the present, the sum total of our pasts. Who I am today is due to what I've done during the past decades. In order to find true inner peace, to be para-ah-dee-ah-tran, we have to accept ourselves unconditionally, *including* the multitude of mistakes we've made. We must forgive ourselves for our human errors."

Winter's heart began to race. Images flashed before her eyes in a tumbling series of jarring scenes.

She saw crowds of hundreds of cheering, applauding, yelling people, as Bright Winter Star stood on stage in her white buckskin dress.

She saw rows of uniformed police officers clearing a path for Bright Winter Star as bodies strained against the human barrier, hands reaching out like claws in an attempt to touch her.

She saw Cliff talking to reporters as she stood one step back and to the side in subservient silence to further enhance the facade of the Indian princess who sang but did not speak.

She saw scenario after scenario, each filling her with self-disgust and shame.

Bessie's words echoed in her mind. *We must forgive ourselves for our human errors.*

No, she thought, not for mistakes of the magnitude she had made. She couldn't just dismiss them out of hand, pat herself on the head and tell herself to forget the past, that what she had done wasn't all that terrible.

No, she had to atone for . . .

"Winter?" Robert said, bringing her back from her tormenting thoughts. "Are you all right? You suddenly look pale."

"What? Oh, yes, I'm fine. Go on with what you were saying, Bessie."

"Well, it's quite simple," the older woman said. "I temporarily lost touch with myself, with who I was and what I really wanted. If I hadn't had that spell with my heart, I would have come back from Old Tucson raving about the wonderful time I'd had, *and* actually believing it by then.

"If the truth be known, the horses smelled dreadful, and when the cowboys shot those guns, I nearly jumped out of my shoes. It was an enchanting place, and certainly made me feel as though I had been transported back to the days of the early west, but it wasn't my cup of tea.

"So, my darlings, I'm calling a halt to my frantic search for adventure. I'm going to reexamine . . . well, me, and discover what it is that I *really* want. First on the agenda is to return to New York and consult my doctor. Whatever conclusions I reach regarding my future plans, I want to be in the best of health to pursue them. I apologize for the distress and upset I've caused either of you, but what's done is done, and it's time to move forward. And that, children, is my story."

"Mother," Robert said, smiling at her warmly, "I think you are one helluva woman. I'm very, *very* proud to be your son."

"Why, thank you, dear. Now! Why don't I make us some lunch? Cooking is definitely on my list of things I truly enjoy doing." She got to her feet. "My, that rain is certainly coming down hard, isn't it?" She started across the room. "I'll call you when it's time to eat. I'll prepare something hot because it's getting quite nippy."

As Bessie left the living room, Winter immediately jumped to her feet. She felt a strange sense of claustrophobia, as though she were being cornered by haunting ghosts and memories of the past.

"Yes, it is damp and chilly, isn't it?" she said, her voice too high and jerky. "A fire. Good idea. We'll have a fire in the fireplace. I have wood in the storeroom and—"

"Winter," Robert interrupted, "What is it?" He stood up, too, and stared at her. "You seem . . . I don't know what you seem, but something is out of sync here. You're jumpy, upset. What's wrong?"

"Wrong?" she repeated, raising her eyebrows. "Well, you see, as much as I admire Bessie's ability to get in touch with her spirit, to be honest with herself and admit to her mistakes, then draw back and regroup, I realize that she's going to be leaving here very soon. That's what's wrong. I'll miss Bessie a great deal."

"Winter, come on, this is me, the man who loves you. There's a lot more distressing you than contemplating how much you'll miss a woman you can keep in constant touch with."

"I'm cold," Winter rushed on. "I get spacey when I'm cold. My blood slugs along to my brain as though it's half frozen. I could turn on the furnace, but it will be much nicer to have a fire. Cozy, you know what I mean?"

He sighed. "All right, I'll drop it for now. Where's the wood?"

"It's in the storeroom beyond the pantry off the kitchen."

Robert pushed through the swinging door to the kitchen, and Winter pressed her fingertips to her lips to stifle the sob rising in her throat.

She was falling apart, she thought, like a rag doll losing its stuffing. The problems she and Robert were facing regarding their future were enough to deal with; but thanks to Bessie's words, the past was looming over her like a horrendous monster.

She turned and opened the screen in front of the fireplace. A two-foot semicircle of Indian tile separated the hearth from the carpet, and off to the right were baskets she had woven. One held newspapers, another contained pinecones she had gathered high in the pine-tree-covered mountains of Oak Creek. The pinecones served in place of kindling. She'd prepare a layer of paper and cones, and have it ready when Robert returned with the juniper logs.

As she started to crumple paper, her glance fell on the love owls. She stood statue-still, hardly breathing. The drumming rain was the only sound in the room, but as she stared intently at the owls, she realized she was straining to hear something else.

As absurd as she knew it to be, she was unable to dismiss the belief that the love owls were attempting to convey a message of vital importance to her.

"Paul Bunyan at your service, ma'am," Robert said, startling her as he came back into the room. One of his arms was curled around a stack of logs. "Oh, and my mother says lunch is ready. I quote, 'Hot, nourishing soup and grilled cheese sandwiches. Perfect for a chilly, rainy day,' end quote. Where do you want these trees?"

Winter gazed vaguely at him, telling herself that if she didn't stop having such ridiculous thoughts about inanimate wax owls, someone would come and cart her away.

"Winter," Robert said, "these aren't toothpicks I'm holding here. These logs are heavy. Where should I put them?"

"Oh. Of course. I'm sorry. Set them on the

edge of the tile there. I'll make a starter base of paper and pinecones."

Within a few minutes, a crackling fire was contributing a welcomed warmth and golden glow to the room.

"Come on, my sweet," Robert said, encircling her shoulders with his arm. "Lunch awaits."

In the eating area of the kitchen, the trio settled in to consume the simple meal. Winter's gaze was drawn time and again to the bay window and the pouring rain.

"Is the storm making you nervous, Winter?" Robert finally asked.

"Oh, no, I enjoy desert storms. Magnificent. That's the word that always comes to mind when I watch one."

Both Bessie and Robert gazed out the window at the thrashing rain and flashing lightning. No one spoke for several minutes.

"Yes," Robert said at last. "You're right. It's so—so intense, as though nature is saying, 'Stop for a minute and get back to basics. Forget the fancy trappings you've surrounded yourself with and remember what's real.'" He looked at Winter almost sheepishly. "That probably didn't make any sense."

"Yes, it did," she said with surprise. "That's it exactly, Robert."

"You amaze me, Bobby," Bessie said. "I've never heard you say anything like that before. All you've ever said about rain is to complain about the inconvenience it causes you."

"Yes, well . . . " He shrugged. "You haven't

cornered the market on changing and growing, Mother."

Bessie smiled. "Obviously not. I think Winter has had a wonderful influence on you. Now, don't scold me for saying this, but if you are seriously involved with Winter, Bobby—"

"Bessie . . ." Winter started.

"I know, dear," Bessie said. "I'm meddling, but it's a privilege of my age. All I'm getting at is that Bobby would be off schedule if the two of you are as smitten as it would appear."

"Five years off schedule," Robert said, chuckling, "but that doesn't bother me for a second. Mother, smitten is a word from another era. Try . . . love. It fits the circumstances."

Winter's eyes widened. "Robert, you agreed not to say—"

"I know," he interrupted, "but it's impossible. We can't carry on a conversation here without everything being laid out on the table. My mother is going back to New York. What if she decides to return to Tucson later? Don't you think she should have all the facts before reaching that decision? Like the tidbit that you wouldn't be here?"

Winter narrowed her eyes. "Oh? Where, pray tell, would I be?"

"With me, of course." He shifted his gaze to Bessie. "Mother, Winter and I are in love, and I've asked her to marry me. We have some little details to work out, but—"

"Little details?" Winter exclaimed. "Is that how you see them? Nagging nuisances that should be quickly dealt with and dismissed?

Well, I have news for you, bub. It isn't going to be that easy."

"Dear me," Bessie said, "for two people newly in love—which absolutely delights me, by the way—you do seem to be rather . . . crabby."

Winter sighed. "Bessie, I felt that Robert and I should work all this out before we said anything to you, but he didn't agree. Anyway, he wants me to give up my home and The Rising Sun, and go where he goes."

"Right," Robert said.

"I see," Bessie said slowly. "And this is causing a major conflict between you two. Am I correct?"

"Yes," Winter said.

"It shouldn't be," Robert said, "but it is. Look, Mother, I don't mean to be rude, but I think we should change the subject. This problem is mine and Winter's to solve. I'm a tad old to be running to Mother with my woes. Winter and I will work this out."

How? Winter wondered. How, Robert?

Bessie looked at Winter for a long moment before speaking again.

"Of course," the older woman said. "Of course you'll work it out, by give-and-take, and compromise."

"Robert doesn't feel that compromise is applicable in all situations," Winter said. "In other words, there are times when one person might have to give one hundred percent."

"This being one of those times?" Bessie asked. "You're to give the one hundred percent, Winter, by leaving your home and The Rising Sun?"

"Yes."

"It's the only way," Robert insisted. "I can't work efficiently from here. I have to move back and forth to the various head offices, just as Father did. There's only so much that can be done by telephone. I need to be there. I'll slowly shift authority so that when Winter and I start a family I can be home more than away, but until then . . . I thought we weren't going to discuss this. Winter and I will find the answers. Now then, Mother, when do you plan to return to New York?"

Again Bessie looked at Winter for a long moment before replying.

"Tomorrow," she finally said. "If I can get a flight out."

"I'll go with you," he said.

"Whatever for?"

"Well, I'd like to hear for myself what your doctor has to say, and I can check in with the New York office while I'm there. I can be back here within a few days."

"And then?" Winter asked.

"You and I will sit down and make our plans."

She got to her feet. "Excuse me for a moment. I need to check on the fire. I imagine it's ready for another log by now." She turned and left the room.

Bessie watched her go, then looked at her son. "Bobby, do you realize what you're asking of Winter?"

He nodded. "I'm asking her to marry me. It's clear enough."

"But, Bobby . . ." Bessie shook her head. "No, I'll keep still."

"I appreciate that. This is between Winter and me."

"Yes," Bessie said quietly. She lifted her spoon, then set it back in place, realizing that she'd suddenly lost her appetite.

Winter stood in front of the fire, her arms wrapped around herself as she stared into the flames. She simply blanked her mind and allowed herself to be mesmerized by those leaping orange flames.

She needed a mental time-out, and clung to it as a drowning man would cling to a life preserver.

"Winter?" Robert said, walking up behind her. "You didn't come back to the table, and you haven't finished your lunch. The soup and sandwich are getting cold."

"I'm not very hungry," she said quietly, her gaze still on the fire.

He placed his hands on her shoulders, then lowered his head and brushed his lips over the soft skin of her throat.

"I'll miss you while I'm in New York," he said, lifting his head again. "I won't be gone any longer than I have to be. When I get back we'll finalize our plans and set things in motion."

Tears misted Winter's eyes, and a sob caught in her throat. "No."

"No? No what?"

She turned to face him, forcing him to drop his hands. "Robert, I love you. I didn't want to love you, but I do. But, oh, God, Robert, I can't do this, do what you're asking of me. *I must stay here.* This is my home. The Rising Sun is my pride and joy. Tucson, the desert, is the place of my personal rising sun that brings peace to my spirit. All that is here. Without those things I'd be lost. Frightened and lost."

"No. Winter, I'd be with you wherever we were. We'd be together, don't you understand? There's nothing to be frightened of, Winter. And lost? What do you mean, lost?"

"I'd lose me, myself, just as I did when I was Bright Winter Star."

"Dammit, I'm not Cliff," he said, nearly shouting. "You'd be my wife, not a robot having your buttons pushed liked before. Winter, you have *got* to let go of the past, so that we can have a future together."

Tears filled her eyes. "No. I'd still be like that robot, as you call it. You can't see it, but you're attempting to manipulate me in your own way, every bit as much as Cliff did in his." She shook her head. "I can't. Not again."

"What are you saying?" he asked gripping her shoulders tightly. "What in the hell are you really saying?"

She lifted her hands as though to touch him, then let her arms drop heavily to her sides.

"I love you," she said, "but I can't marry you. I'm sorry if . . . sorry if I hurt you, Robert, but . . . I have to stay here, and you can't stay here, so I think it would be best if you left now . . . before there . . . is any more . . . pain."

"Winter?" he asked, searching her face. "You

can't mean it. No, Winter, don't do this to us. We just found each other, and you're throwing it all away. We'll be happy, I swear to God we will, even if you're not in this house, in this city, owning that store. There *is* a world out there, Winter, just waiting for us to enjoy it together. Please, stop and realize what you're doing to us. Let the past die so that our future can really be born. Winter? Please?"

Tears streamed down her face. "Good-bye, Robert."

Disbelief flashed across his face, then anger; finally, pain settled in the depths of his eyes. He stared at her for a long, long moment before turning and walking across the room, picking up his jacket as he went. A moment later he stepped out into the raging storm, without even having put his jacket on as a shield against the cold, driving rain.

Bessie walked into the living room just as the front door slammed shut. She turned to look questioningly at Winter, who buried her face in her hands and wept.

Nine

Winter stood by the front windows of The Rising Sun and watched the water in the courtyard fountain spray up and up, then fall in a graceful cascade.

The late-afternoon sun was still bright enough to dance over the water, creating a glorious, rainbow-colored spectacle that looked like a million sparkling diamonds. Several people stood by the fountain taking pictures, attempting to capture its beauty on film.

Winter sighed and turned from the window. In the past, the sight of the fountain had never failed to bring a smile to her lips. But not today. In the ten days since Robert had walked out of her home and into the cold rain, her smiles had been forced, produced only when customers entered the store.

Once again that last scene with Robert replayed in her mental vision. And once again, she felt the ache of unshed tears.

Winter Holt, she admonished herself, stop it. She'd been over it and over it, seeking a solution to what had torn her and Robert apart. She'd found none. He wanted her to go, she knew she had to stay, and that was that.

And she missed him so much that the cold fist of loneliness seemed to have a permanent, painful grip on her heart.

She'd spoken on the telephone with Bessie twice since the older woman had returned to New York. She had seen her doctor, Bessie had told Winter, and a long walk was now part of her daily routine. She'd been put on a diet that forbade sugary desserts and all cholesterol-producing foods, but had been declared to be in good health in the overall picture.

She was going to be second-in-command in organizing the Christmas dance at The Plaza, leaving the majority of the endless details to someone else, she'd chattered on to Winter. She'd inquired as to Winter's well-being, but had not mentioned Robert's name.

Dear Bessie, Winter thought. She'd been caught in the middle of a hopeless situation between Winter and Robert, and had apparently decided it was best to say nothing in reference to it.

Winter looked at her watch, and realized that Siki and Dulcie would be arriving at any moment to take over the evening hours at the store.

Oh, Lord, she thought dismally, she didn't want to go home to her empty house. What had once been a welcoming haven had turned into an echoing, empty series of rooms that seemed to taunt her with the knowledge that Robert was gone forever.

But she was miserable at The Rising Sun too. This was where she'd first met Robert, and the store reverberated with memories of their first kiss and their laughing conversation about sheep dung pots.

There was nowhere to go, nowhere to hide, from haunting, heartbreaking remembrances of Robert Stone.

The door opened, to the accompaniment of the tinkling bells, and Winter was grateful she was no longer alone with her tormenting thoughts. The smile she produced disappeared instantly as Dulcie came in without Siki.

"Is something wrong?" she asked anxiously. "Where's Siki?"

"Barry just took her to the hospital," Dulcie said, smiling. "The baby has decided to arrive a couple of weeks early. Siki's water broke, and off they went. It was quicker to just come on over here rather than call you."

"Is Siki upset?" Winter asked.

"Heavens, no," Dulcie said, laughing. "She's as cool as a cucumber. Now, Barry, he's a wreck. I'm telling you, Winter, the guy has lost it. The last thing I heard him say was that he'd changed his mind, he couldn't handle this, and the baby would just have to stay put where it was. Siki slugged him on the arm."

Winter laughed. "Which is why women have the babies and not men."

"True. Listen, I feel confident about running the store alone. Siki said I had it all down pat. It's up to you, though, Winter. You're not going to hurt my feelings if you stick around."

"No, no, you don't need me." Did anyone? she wondered. "I'll go home, have some dinner, then drive over to the hospital and keep Barry company. I don't think St. Mary's is ready for Barry Nanchez in a state of panic."

"Good thought," Dulcie said. "Be sure and keep me posted."

As Winter drove home, she absently wondered what she should eat for dinner. She'd had little appetite since Robert's exodus, and usually brought a book to the table with her and ended up reading more than eating.

She pulled into her driveway, glanced at the house, then did a double take as she slammed on the brakes. Her eyes widened as she stared at her front yard.

There was a tepee in her yard, she thought incredulously. There was a huge, honest-to-goodness, Indians-live-here tepee right there. And to further convince her that she'd totally lost her mind, a small camp fire was burning in front of the tepee.

She turned off the ignition to the van and opened the door, praying that her trembling legs would support her. She walked tentatively forward, her gaze fixed on the structure, which refused, despite her severe mental directives, to disappear.

She stopped about three feet in front of the tepee, her purse clutched to her breasts like a security blanket.

"Hello?" she called nervously. "Hello?"

She jerked in surprise as the flap of the tepee was flung back, then gasped as Robert Stone emerged. He straightened and folded his arms across his chest. He was wearing faded jeans and a bulky fisherman's sweater. Her mouth dropped open to form an astonished, soundless, 'Oh.'

"Howdy," he said, then frowned. "No, that's not right. How about 'How'? Forget it. We'll settle for "Hi, how's life?'" A smile tugged at his lips, "Close your mouth, Winter, you're going to catch flies."

She snapped her mouth shut, drew in a wobbly breath, then attempted to speak. She was still wondering if she was imagining this entire scene.

"What . . ." she started, but her voice was a mere squeak. She stopped and tried again. "What are you doing here? And why is there a tepee in my yard?" Oh, he was so beautiful, her Robert, and she loved him. She'd missed him and wanted to fling herself into his arms. That was *not* a good idea, though. If she really was cuckoo and Robert was a mirage, said flinging would accomplish nothing more than landing her on her nose on the ground.

"It's very simple, Winter," he answered her. "I have just spent the worst ten days of my life since leaving here, and I won't even get into how lousy the nights have been. My own mother was no comfort to me, either. She called me a stuffed shirt and a stubborn prig, which did nothing for my morale, then refused to speak to me until I'd slowed down and had a very serious discussion with *myself*."

"Oh," Winter said, then for the life of her couldn't think of another thing to say.

"So, I talked to myself at great length," Robert went on, "and I must admit the names I ended up calling myself made my mother seem polite. I've been very narrow-minded and unfair to you, Winter. I dismissed everything that was precious to you because it didn't seem as important as what I do. That was wrong, and I'm sorry. I'm also very deeply in love with you, and I intend to do everything within my power to convince you to marry me."

"But . . ."

"I could have checked into the hotel," he continued, "and come beating on your door to deliver all my grand declarations of intent, but I decided that action was required here. In order to show you that I truly do respect your lifestyle, your home, The Rising Sun store, and the rising sun of your personal inner peace, I've moved into that world in this tepee."

She eyed him warily. "You've flipped your switch, Stone."

"Impossible, Holt," he shot back. "This tepee doesn't have electricity. Hence, no switches."

"Oh, for Pete's sake. Robert—"

"There *is* a compromise to be found somewhere in this mess, but it will take both of us, *together*, to find it. Now, don't get all in a huff and turn that temper of yours loose on me, because I have to say this. It's *your* turn to have a long talk with yourself. You have to decide what your priorities are, and if you intend to continue to allow your past to dictate your future. While you're doing all that mental inventory, all that dusting and cleaning of your mind, I'll be right here in my tepee waiting to have a powwow when you're ready."

"Dusting and cleaning of my mind?" she repeated, before a funny near-hysterical giggle escaped from her lips.

"Hey, that was a very profound way of putting it, madam," he said, appearing very pleased with himself. "Would you care for a tour of my abode?"

"What? Oh, I can't right now. I have to go to the hospital to have a baby."

He gaped at her. "I beg your pardon?"

"No, no, not me. What I mean is, Siki is having her baby."

"No kidding? That's great. Okay, I'll go with you. Just give me a minute to put out my camp fire here."

"Dandy," Winter said, waving one hand breezily in the air. "I have to go inside to . . . I think I was going to have dinner, but forget that. I'll be back in a minute."

"Right."

"Robert, humor me." She tentatively extended a finger and pressed it to the center of his chest. He stared down at her finger, and so did she. "You're real," she said. "This is actually happening. Fancy that." She pulled back her finger, looked at the end of it, then turned and started toward the house.

"Whoa!" Robert yelled. "Halt!"

She stopped. He walked over to her and carefully settled his hands at her waist.

"I can't have you thinking your imagination has gone haywire," he said, gazing into her eyes. "I'm here, I'm real, and I'm very much in love with you." He lowered his head toward hers. "There is no doubt about it."

A delicious shiver of anticipation rippled through Winter, and then Robert's mouth was on hers, his tongue parting her lips to seek and find her tongue.

Oh, Robert, she thought dreamily, her lashes drifting down. He was really, truly here.

She savored his taste, his aroma of aftershave, fresh air, and tangy mesquite wood smoke. She relished the feel of his strong hands at her waist, and the soft pressure of his lips on hers. Heat swirled deep within her, and desire burst free like a wild bird.

He ended the kiss and spoke, his lips on hers. "Do you believe now that I'm really here?" he asked.

"Yes," she whispered, slowly opening her eyes.

"Do you know that I love you?"

"Yes."

"Do you love me?"

"Yes. Oh, yes."

"Will you dust and clean your mind?"

"I'll vacuum it, I promise."

"We'll find the answers, Winter. If we do it

together, stay united like our love owls, we can do it."

"Yes."

"Good. Let's go have Siki's baby."

"Yes."

He dropped his hands, and she walked to the house, her legs somewhat unsteady.

"I love you, Winter Holt," Robert said quietly as she went inside. "And I need you with me forever."

In her bedroom, Winter changed into jeans and a burnt orange sweater, going through the motions by rote as her mind dwelled on Robert and all he'd said to her.

Oh, how she loved him and, oh, how she'd missed him and, oh, how she wanted him, wanted to mesh her body with his in the exquisite lovemaking that was theirs alone.

She rushed back down the hall and into the living room, then stopped as her eyes collided with the love owls on the mantel.

"Speak to me," she whispered. "I know you're trying to, I just know it. Please send your message louder so that I can hear it."

She waited a moment, then tore her gaze from the pair of birds and raced out the front door.

The traffic was especially heavy on the way to the hospital, and Robert had to concentrate on driving the car he'd rented. Still, he couldn't help thinking about the lovely woman sitting beside him.

He smiled inwardly as he remembered Winter's astonished expression when she discovered him and his tepee in her front yard. And thank heavens she hadn't ordered him to pack up and haul himself out of there. She'd promised, too, to have a lengthy discussion with herself.

The past ten days and nights, he freely admitted, had been agony. He'd felt as though he'd lost a part of who he was and was walking around in a half-empty shell, pretending he was the Robert Stone everyone knew.

He'd been forced to face some very unflattering facts about himself and the way he conducted his life. Then he'd gotten on a plane and come back to Winter. His Winter, his love, the woman who could give depth and meaning to his life.

"Winter," he said, glancing over at her, "while I was gone, I reviewed in my mind the capabilities of each of the top people in my offices around the world. They're very competent, intelligent men and women. While there are still certain transactions I should handle personally, I don't need to be there as much as I have been."

"Go on," Winter said as hope began to grow inside her.

"I had a report prepared for me regarding the investment possibilities in Arizona—the available land, the economy, that type of data."

"And?"

"There's potential here for many endeavors.

What I'm proposing as my part of our compromise is that I make Tucson my home base of operation."

"But you don't like the desert, Robert."

"Not true. I didn't give the desert a chance. I took one look around, decided it was stark, bare, and hot, and rejected it flat out. You showed me the beauty of a desert storm, and I have a lot more to learn. It's time I stopped long enough to appreciate the gift of a gorgeous sunset, for example."

"Oh, Robert, that's wonderful. I—"

He shook his head. "No, now wait. We're talking compromise here, remember? Give and take, fifty-fifty. I would *still* have to travel. Not as much, but some, and I'd want you with me. Don't comment on this now, but when you're dusting and cleaning your mind, I want you to have the whole picture."

He stopped at a red light and met her gaze.

"You have to decide if you're willing to step out of your safe world at times, leave your home, let Siki and others tend to The Rising Sun store and the sheep dung pots until you return."

"But . . ."

"Just listen, okay? That's what would be happening on the surface. What it would really mean is that you've freed yourself of the pain of the past, and are ready to share a future with me."

The light turned green, and Robert turned his attention back to his driving.

"Don't say anything," he went on, "just think about it. And take all the time you need. There's the hospital up ahead. Does Siki want a boy or a girl?"

"What? Oh, she doesn't care. She just wants a healthy baby. Barry is more inclined to follow Apache traditions, so he's hoping for a girl."

"Really? I would have thought first priority would be a son—a potential leader of the people, or a warrior."

"No, Apaches have always hoped for firstborn children to be girls. Chiricahua Apache women share an equal voice and power with men. The skills and wisdom of a woman are held in high esteem."

"Interesting," Robert said. "And I thoroughly agree with the theory. There's a certain half-Apache woman who is at the top of my list of importance too."

Winter smiled, but that smile soon faded as she replayed in her mind what Robert had suggested should be her half of the compromise. His echoing words were accompanied by a chilling sense of fear.

A little over three hours later, Siki and Barry Nanchez were the proud parents of a six-pound seven-ounce girl. She was, the exuberant Barry declared, the most beautiful, absolutely most perfect baby ever born.

Siki had been calm and brave, Barry said, while he himself had nearly passed out on the floor of the delivery room. He was off to say good night to his Siki, but if Winter and Robert hurried, the nurse had agreed to give them a quick peek at the infant before drawing the curtains over the nursery window.

"Kiss Siki for me," Winter said, smiling at Barry. "And congratulations to you both."

"I'm the happiest man in the world," the handsome new father said. "Go see the baby. You won't believe how beautiful she is."

"Okay, okay," Winter said, laughing, "we're going. Oh, what did you name her? Siki said you were still discussing names the last time I asked her."

"Her name," Barry said proudly, "is Robin. Robin Winter Nanchez."

"Oh, Barry, I'm so honored. I had no idea that you . . . I don't know what to say."

"Go see her," he said, then turned and sprinted down the hall.

"Robin Winter Nanchez," she said softly. "What a lovely gift Siki and Barry have given me."

Robert draped his arm around her shoulders. "Come on. I'm eager to have a look at your namesake."

Outside the nursery, Winter printed the name Nanchez with chalk on a small slate and held it up to the window. A nurse smiled, nodded, then mouthed "Two minutes." A few moments later, she stepped close to the glass, a small bundle wrapped in a pink blanket nestled in the crook of her arm. She drew the blanket partially away.

"Oh," Winter said, with a wistful sigh. "Oh, Robert, look at her. Isn't she beautiful?"

"Yes," he said, "she really is. Lord, she's small. I'd be scared to death I'd break her if I tried to hold her. She sure has a lot of hair, doesn't she?"

"Indian babies usually do," Winter said absently, unable to tear her gaze from the baby.

Robert and I, she thought dreamily, *would have a darling baby like Robin Winter, with silky black hair and skin the color of a sun-kissed peach. Robert and I, together, would create . . .*

. . . A miracle, Robert thought. *That baby is a miracle, the evidence of Siki and Barry's love for each other. The baby Winter and I could have would have black hair and golden skin, and be every bit as beautiful as Robin Winter. What a mind-boggling thought to realize that the fabulous lovemaking I share with Winter could produce a . . .*

. . . A baby, a baby, Winter thought. *A child who is a part of Robert, a part of me. Oh, Robert, I love you so much . . .*

. . . I love you, Winter. The future can be ours if you'll just let it be. Please, Winter, leave the past and come into the present and the future with me.

The nurse moved back, smiled and waved to Winter and Robert, then nodded to someone off to the side and out of their view. The curtain slid shut over the window.

Winter and Robert didn't move. They stood like statues, staring at the curtain. Robert finally cleared his throat.

"Well," he said, "Robin Winter Nanchez is a heart-stealer already. She's really something."

"Yes. Yes, she is," Winter said.

"Are you hungry now? Do you want to stop on the way home for something to eat?"

"No, thank you, I'm not hungry. I couldn't eat." She turned and started down the corridor.

Robert fell in step beside her, and neither spoke again as they left the hospital and drove to Winter's house. Their thoughts were turned inward, lost in the mazes in their minds.

Darkness had fallen and stars twinkled in the heavens as Robert stopped in front of the tepee. He hunkered down to rebuild his fire, and a few minutes later a small, warming blaze burned in the circle of rocks. He stood again and met Winter's gaze.

"Well, good night," he said.

"Robert, are you really going to stay out here?"

He nodded. "Yes, I am. I have a sleeping bag in there, food, everything I need. I think it's important that I do more than just talk about my intentions. I need to show you that I'm sincere, that I mean every word."

"But . . ."

"Go into the house, okay? If I so much as touch you, Winter, I'm going to blow this to smithereens. I want you . . . Lord knows how much I want to make love with you, but this isn't the time."

She looked at him for a long moment, then nodded. Turning, she walked slowly into the house, feeling suddenly drained, and barely able to put one foot in front of the other.

In the living room, she switched on one lamp,

then crossed the room to stare at the birds on the mantel. Time lost meaning as she stood there, hardly breathing, only listening, listening, to the message from the symbols of eternal love.

Just after midnight, Robert gave up his futile attempt to sleep and left the tepee. He sat on the ground and added another piece of mesquite to the glowing embers of his fire.

Moments later, flames licked heavenward, warming him, making it unnecessary for him to put on his jacket over his fisherman's sweater.

He was exhausted, from jet lag and from the sleepless nights he'd endured after arriving in New York. But he was too wired to relax. Everything, *everything*, was riding on what Winter would discover when she looked closely at herself and faced her inner demons.

He closed his eyes and squeezed the bridge of his nose. If only he could sleep, he mused, escape for a few hours from the turmoil and, yes, the fear that haunted him.

Suddenly he heard a noise he couldn't identify. His head snapped up, and he squinted, trying to see through the flames and smoke of the fire into the darkness beyond.

Then he heard it—the melodic sound of Winter singing.

"I cry in the darkness . . . my tears fall like rain . . . but I weep not from heartbreak . . . nor sorrow or pain."

His heart thundered as he got to his feet. An

image appeared in the mist of the smoke and the wavy heat of the flames.

Winter. Moving slowly toward him in a white buckskin dress adorned with a multitude of beads, her hair a shiny cascade, she sang on.

"My heart sings, my soul sings . . . my spirit is free . . . of ghosts of past shadows . . . that long taunted me."

Too enraptured by her beauty and her voice to move, Robert listened intently to every precious word she sang.

"The rising sun . . . the rising sun."

She stopped just beyond the fire and met his gaze. Tears glistened in her eyes, and her voice broke when she began the next verse.

"It's not just a place now . . . within which to hide . . . it's part of my being . . . warm courage inside."

Robert gave up the struggle against his emotions, and tears filled his own eyes.

"The rising sun . . . the rising sun . . . I reach out my hand to . . . the man of my heart . . . and know that 'til death speaks . . . we never shall part.

"Together we'll travel . . . but wherever we roam . . . joy will surround us . . . and make it our home.

"And our rising sun . . . our rising sun . . . our rising sun."

Her voice faded away, and she took one step closer to him.

"Robert," she said, "forgive me for not having the wisdom to forgive myself. This dress belonged to Bright Winter Star. I kept just one to remind myself of what a fool I had been, how shamefully I'd betrayed myself and my people."

She drew in a shuddering breath. "But now I've let the past go, put it to rest at long last. Bright Winter Star, this dress, that whole era of my life, doesn't torment me anymore. It's all a part of who I was then, so that I could become the Winter Holt you fell in love with now. Our rising sun . . . *ours*, Robert, will be wherever we are together. I love you. The compromise that you offered was perfect, and I accept your plan with a glad heart. Para-ah-dee-ah-tran, my beloved Robert Stone, forever."

Robert stepped around the fire to her, and cradled her face in his hands. He made no attempt to hide his tears.

"Oh, Winter," he said, his voice husky with emotion, "thank God. I don't know what I would have done if I'd lost you. I love you so much, I need you with me for the rest of my life. I want to make love to you and create our baby girl. Ah, Winter, *you* are my rising sun."

He captured her mouth in a searing kiss that spoke of fading memories of pain and fear, of looking forward instead of back, of walking side by side rather than alone.

And the kiss ignited a desire that flared as brightly as the flames leaping from the fire in front of the tepee.

Robert raised his head and met Winter's gaze. "I want you, Winter," he said. "But I need you, too, and I love you. What made you change your mind? I was afraid, just so damn scared, that your ghosts were going to prove stronger than the power of my love for you. What happened?"

"I listened. I listened and I heard what they said."

"They? They who?"

"It was the . . ." She stopped speaking and smiled up at him, love shining in the depths of her dark eyes. "Do you recognize that sound?"

He cocked his head slightly to one side. "Owls. It's . . . Yes, there are two of them, calling and answering each other, as though they're talking."

"Yes."

"Winter, wait a minute. Are you saying that the love owls, *our* love owls, spoke to you and . . ."

"That's what I'll tell our children and our grandchildren, Robert. Then I'll sing them the song of the rising sun."

He brushed his lips over hers. "That's fine. The Stone family will have its very own legend. I like that. Let's go inside, Winter, because I intend to make love to you for hours, and I'm not cut out for this roughing-it-on-the-ground business."

They extinguished the fire, then with their arms around each other, they entered the house.

"You go ahead," Winter said. "I just want to shut off this light."

"I'll be waiting for you," he said, and walked down the hall.

Winter crossed the room and smiled gently, wisely, as she looked at the empty place on the mantel where the love owls had been. She shifted her gaze to the window and envisioned the dark night beyond the drapes.

"Thank you," she whispered. "Thank you so much."

Far, far in the distance came an owl's mellow hoot, followed by another.

Winter blew a kiss into the air, then turned and walked down the hallway, quickening her step as she went to Robert Stone, the man she would love for all time, her other half, her rising sun.

THE EDITOR'S CORNER

Come join the celebration next month as LOVESWEPT reaches an important milestone—the publication of LOVESWEPT #500! The journey has been exceptionally rewarding, and we're proud of each book we've brought you along the way. Our commitment to put the LOVESWEPT imprint only on the best romances is unwavering, and we invite you to share with us the trip to LOVESWEPT #1000. One step toward that goal is the lineup of six fabulous reading treasures we have in store for you.

Please give a rousing welcome to Linda Jenkins and her first LOVESWEPT, **TOO FAR TO FALL,** #498. Linda already has five published romances to her credit, and you'll soon see why we're absolutely thrilled to have her. **TOO FAR TO FALL** features one rugged hunk of a hero, but Trent Farraday is just too gorgeous for Miranda Hart's own good. His sexy grin makes her tingle to her toes when he appears at her door to fix a clogged drain. How can a woman who's driven to succeed be tempted by a rogue who believes in taking his time? With outrageous tenderness, Trent breaches Miranda's defenses and makes her taste the fire in his embrace. Don't miss this wonderful romance by one of our New Faces of '91!

In **THE LADY IN RED,** LOVESWEPT #499, Fayrene Preston proves why that color has always symbolized love and passion. Reporter Cassidy Stuart is clad in a slinky red-sequined sheath when she invades Zach Bennett's sanctuary, and the intriguing package ignites his desire. Only his addictive kisses make Cassidy confess that she's investigating the story about his immensely successful toy company being under attack. Zach welcomes the lovely sleuth into his office and as they try to uncover who's determined to betray him, he sets out on a thrilling seduction of Cassidy's guarded heart. As always, Fayrene Preston writes with spellbinding sensuality, and the wonderful combination of mystery and romance makes this book a keeper.

Glenna McReynolds sets the stage for an enchanting and poignant tale with **MOONLIGHT AND SHADOWS,** LOVESWEPT #500. Jack Hudson blames the harvest moon for driving him crazy enough to draw Lila Singer into his arms the night they meet and to kiss her breathless! He has no idea the beautiful young widow has relinquished her dreams of love. Lila knows there could only be this sensual heat between them—they have nothing else in common. Jack has never backed down from a challenge, and convincing Lila to take a chance on more than one special night together is the sweetest dare of all. A beautiful love story that you won't be able to put down.

Guaranteed to heat your blood is **THE SECRET LIFE OF ELIZABETH McCADE,** LOVESWEPT #501 by Peggy Webb. Black Hawk burns with the same restless fever that Elizabeth McCade keeps a secret, and when this legendary Chickasaw leader hides from his enemies in her house, he bewitches her senses and makes her promise to keep him safe. But nothing can protect her from the uncontrollable desire that flares between them. Elizabeth is haunted by painful memories, while Hawk has his own dark shadows to face, and both must overcome fears before they can surrender to ecstasy. Together these two create a blazing inferno of passion that could melt the polar ice caps!

Marvelous talent Laura Taylor joins our fold with the sensational **STARFIRE,** LOVESWEPT #502. With his irresistible looks, business superstar Jake Stratton is every woman's fantasy, but professor Libby Kincaid doesn't want to be his liaison during his visiting lecturer series—even though his casual touch makes her ache with a hunger she can't name. Jake's intrigued by this vulnerable beauty who dresses in shapeless clothes and wears her silky hair in a tight bun. But Libby doesn't want to want any man, and capturing her may be the toughest maneuver of Jake's life. A real winner from another one of our fabulous New Faces of '91!

Finally, from the magical pen of Deborah Smith, we have **HEART OF THE DRAGON,** LOVESWEPT #503. Set in exotic Thailand, this fabulous love story features Kash Santelli—remember him from *The Silver Fox and the Red Hot Dove*? Kash is prepared to frighten Rebecca Brown off, believing she's a greedy schemer out to defraud her half sister, but once he meets her, nothing about the minister's daughter suggests deception. Indeed, her feisty spirit and alluring innocence make him want to possess her. When Rebecca finds herself in the middle of a feud, Kash must help—and Rebecca is stunned by her reckless desire for this powerful, enigmatic man. Riveting, captivating—everything you've come to expect from Deborah Smith . . . and more.

And (as if this weren't enough!) be sure to look for the four spectacular novels coming your way from FANFARE, where you'll find only the best in women's fiction. **REAP THE WIND** by bestselling author Iris Johansen is the thrilling conclusion to the unforgettable Wind Dancer trilogy. **THE SWANSEA DESTINY** by much-loved Fayrene Preston is the long-awaited prequel to her SwanSea series from LOVESWEPT. Critically acclaimed Virginia Lynn delivers another humorous and exciting Wild West historical in **CUTTER'S WOMAN,** and Pamela Morsi follows the success of her first book with **COURTING MISS HATTIE,** a very touching story of a spinster who finds true love.

What a terrific month of reading in store for you from LOVESWEPT and FANFARE!

With warmest wishes,

Nita Taublib

Nita Taublib
Associate Publisher, LOVESWEPT
Publishing Associate, FANFARE
Bantam Books
666 Fifth Avenue
New York, NY 10103

"Ms. Gill taps into our deepest emotions in this provocative love story, proving herself skillfully adept at touching our hearts." — Rave Reviews

Bad Billy Culver

By Judy Gill

Betrayal . . . a dark secret . . . a love that would outlast slander and time and taboo. . .

Billy Culver grew up poor, handsome as the devil -- and twice as bad. Arlene Lambert grew up in a home full of the security and elegance old money could provide. And she loved the housekeeper's son. Suddenly, scorned and condemned for a transgression he did not commit, Billy was driven out of town.

Now, rich and powerful and determined, Bad Billy Culver is back -- and dead set on getting revenge. When he confronts Arlene, he is tormented by guilt . . . renewed feelings of desire . . . and echoes of love. Arlene has never stopped loving Billy. But it is a love she cannot act on -- because of a secret so profound, so shameful that she will lose love itself to keep it from coming to light.

"This is incredible reading. Both protagonists are so real you can touch them . . . . A definite must!" --*Rendezvous*

THE SYMBOL OF GREAT WOMEN'S FICTION FROM BANTAM
On sale now at your local bookstore.

AN 335 - 9/91